COCKY ROCKSTAR: GABRIEL

FALEENA HOPKINS

HOP HOP PUBLICATIONS

COCKY ROCKSTAR:

GABRIEL COCKER

I believe in love at first sight. You want that connection, and then you want some problems.

— KEANU REEVES

PAIGE

"That's right, ladies, you could win a date with your favorite singer heartthrob, *Gabriel Cocker!*"

Shelby raises the volume. "Paige, listen!"

"Sometime in the next hour we'll play Gabriel's hit song, *Existence,* so call in when you hear it! Eleventh caller wins!"

I snap the radio off with a roll of my eyes. "Nobody actually wins those things."

"Somebody does. Why not you?" she asks as I straighten the yoga pants bearing the pretty *Om This* logo while worrying to myself.

When Bobby resurfaces I'll confront him.

I can't believe he did this to us.

If we don't have rent by Monday...

We'll be on the streets.

I'm sure he'll come home tonight.

It's going to be...

"Shit!" my best friend shouts, staring at the calendar. "Nobody has signed up for my class! Am I doing something wrong? There are twenty-two students for yours and five reserved for mine! Why!?"

"Did you check the bathrooms?"

"Yes, the janitor did a bang-up job. We can now eat off the toilet seats."

Under my breath I remind myself, "Have to hang a new guidelines note on the back door. The old one is torn."

"You didn't answer my question."

I mumble, "Put on the Zen playlist, Shelbs. People will be here at any minute. No commercials during class."

She shouts, "PAIGE!"

Startled I drop the pants. "Jeez! What?"

"Where are you right now? I've been talking to you and you're not listening!"

Fantastic.

How am I supposed to teach classes like this?

If I'm going to survive the day I'd better focus.

Rolling my dark brown hair into a tight bun I blink at her. "I'm sorry, what were you saying?"

"That you have *way* more people signed up. Look!" She whips the iPad around and points to the calendar. "You. Me. Twenty-two. Five. Huge difference! Is my teaching really that terrible?"

"No! You're amazing." She doesn't catch the lavender incense I toss at her. It goes clattering to the ground as I insist, "I'm personally addicted to your classes!"

"They apparently do *not* agree with you. These signups don't lie."

"You're a great teacher and you know it. Pick up the incense."

Writing today's date on a fresh piece of paper for the mailing list she shakes her head. "I'm not a healer like you, Paige. You make stress go away just by the sound of your soothing voice."

Staring at her I sigh, "That's ironic."

"What is?"

That I can make other people's stress go away, yet here I am with knots in my stomach.

"Nothing. Pick up the incense!"

"You threw it." At my expression she throws up her hands. "Okay! I'm getting it."

I walk to the front and flip the sign over in the window from *'Love and Light'* to *'All Are Welcome,'* pausing as I see the ominously dark parking lot with black polka dots appearing on the asphalt.

Touching the glass I moan, "No!"

We get paid by the number of students we teach.

I need every single one of them attending today.

No cancellations.

Is life always going to be this hard?

Shelby asks, "What's wrong?"

"The clouds are coming in like the Devil sent them. Half our students won't show up now."

"That means I'll have two-point-five people?! How am I going to teach half a human?"

"You're being ridiculous. Look at your lunchtime class. Is there an increase there?"

She runs her finger around the screen and tilts her head. "Okay, I've got thirty-three people for it. I'll stop whining. Oh, listen! I haven't heard this song in ages!" She turns up the volume. An old Simone Ross-Taylor hit fills the air with an amazing dance beat. "God, whatever happened to her?"

"I read she got married and had kids, moved to Spain."

"He wouldn't let her sing?"

"No, he did. I think she just didn't want to grow old in front of her fans."

"Tragic!" Shelby climbs on the stool that lives behind the register, and starts wiggling her ass and arms, blonde curls bouncing. "Dance with me, Paige!"

"I'm not in the mood to dance," I grumble, but my hips are moving despite my worries.

She shouts, "Woot! Woot!" and spins her head around. The silliness is infectious so I grab a purple yoga mat from our Sale rack and dance like it's my tango partner. "Break it down, Paige! That's right! Do it! Yeah baby! Break it down!"

The bells twinkle as three of our Monday morning regulars hurry in leaving raindrops reaching for them.

But do we stop?

Hells to the no!

Nisse takes one look and laughs, "Is this the kind of day we're having?"

While I dip my purple lover, Shelby calls to Nisse and the other students over the music, "It is now!"

Of course our wild Lisa jumps in immediately. That woman is up for anything. "I so need to dance, you don't even know."

Michelle sets down her things with a shrug, "Screw it, I'm in," and starts grooving without inhibition.

Outside, the rain is picking up at a feverish pace. More students catapult themselves into our store to escape it. Angela, Liz, Ruby and Pam each brush water off their hair while reacting to our impromptu dance party.

Angela cries out, "Where's the wine?!"

Liz laughs, "She's not joking."

"I am totally joking!"

Ruby roll her eyes. "I could use a drink after getting my kids to school."

Pam mutters, "Right? Getting Henry in his car-seat was like wrestling a gator."

Everyone laughs, shaking their bodies freely and without a need to be 'good' as the last few stragglers hurry in – Ms. Bauer, Josephine and Brenda.

Brenda grabs Josephine's hand to make her swing dance, modifying elaborate moves for the compact space.

I call over, "Wow! Look at you, Brenda!"

"I used to teach Swing at the YMCA!"

Josephine is laughing. "You're amazing. Will you give my husband lessons?"

"Honey, don't tempt me. We're all friends here!"

We all whoop at her joke.

The only one who refuses to join in is Ms. Bauer. Honestly, that she even attends class at all is a mystery to me, much less the three days a week as she religiously does. She's never spoken to anyone. The only greeting I've ever received from her is a grunt.

Does she dampen our spirits?

Not one little bit.

When it switches to another song, Shelby and I lock eyes and holler, "Can we get a *hell yeah*?"

They all raise their arms and shout, "Hell yeah!" except for Ms. Bauer.

And we dance that whole song, too.

As it nears its end I glance to the clock. Exactly three minutes ago we were supposed to have started our classes.

I call out, "Shelbs, much as I hate to say this, turn it off. We have to begin. Some of you guys work right after this?"

Groans all around because yes, everyone has obligations whether it's work or community philanthropy, or just cleaning the damn house before their kids tear it up again.

Nisse announces, "My babysitter charges double

when I'm late. It's my fault! The clock and I aren't friends."

Michelle suggests, "You really should call Terrianne. She's very fair and wouldn't penalize you for that."

Lisa tells everyone, "I adore Terrianne! Last time she babysat for my boys she brought home-baked banana bread. She's amazing!"

Nisse shakes her head. "It's my kids! *We love Jax P-J,* they always cry out. That's Jackie's nickname. Cute huh? What can I do?"

"Be on time."

"Nope."

Shelby shouts, "No paying double!" as her fingers reach for the dial to switch to our Zen playlist.

All of sudden a horrendous noise explodes in our lobby-store as Ms. Bauer hack coughs like crazy, calling everyone's attention to her because it is loud and hideous. She bends over with her drink canister held far away like whatever was in it poisoned her.

I hurry over to the poor woman as her face goes dark red. "Raise your arms over your head, Ms. Bauer! Your lungs need space. Come on! Arms up!" I grab them and hold them high. As a thank you I get a fresh round of hacking right in my face. But it worked, and she starts to calm down.

Shelby shouts, "Hey, Listen!" She's pointing at the radio, her cell phone pressed tightly against her ear.

The DJ says, "Hello! Tell me your name!"

Shelby says, "This is Paige Miller calling!"

My jaw drops.

"Well, Paige Miller, can you guess what caller you are?"

Shelby asks, "The eleventh one?"

He does a dramatic pause and bellows, "That's right! You're the eleventh caller, Paige! You've won a date with Gabriel Cocker, plus two tickets to his concert this Friday night!"

Our students start screaming their brains out.

Most are happily married.

Doesn't matter. He's that hot.

Ruby shouts, "Oh my God! Oh my God!"

Brenda makes monkey sounds through cupped hands.

Stunned I say, "I didn't even hear his song come on."

The DJ laughs through the speakers, "We have some Gabriel fans there with you, Paige?"

"We sure do!" Shelby grins then holds the phone out for more hooting and shouting from all the women here.

That is, everyone but Ms. Bauer...and me.

"Paige, your friends must think you are one lucky girl. Now hold on the line and someone will collect your information. And to the rest of you Gabriel fans listening to K.L.C.K. we've got more tickets coming up to give away, every hour on the hour!"

The volume of *Existence* increases back to normal as Shelby bounces around, waiting for the radio station to take her off hold.

I am speechless.

Ms. Bauer for the very first time, isn't.

"You *bitch!*"

She storms out.

We all stare after her and Angela mutters, "What the hell was that about!?"

Brenda cocks an eyebrow with a knowing look. "The people who won't dance are the ones who need it most."

They disappear.

I hear someone announce from the other room, "I can't dance but I still do it!"

"You have to dance," someone else mutters. "It's mandatory for living."

I'm alone again with my best friend who just did the stupidest thing without my permission and without knowing about the troubles in my life. Stunned I whisper, "Oh my God, Shelby, why did you do that?"

"You'll thank me later," she smirks.

GABRIEL

"*I* am not looking forward to this."

Maggie looks up from her phone, thumbs still typing as she asks, "Is it your dad?"

"No, my twin brother." Swiping to answer I get off the couch and walk away. "Elijah, don't even. I know what you're about to say."

His voice is apologetic, but not sorry enough. "I can't make it to the concert."

"I fucking knew it!" I shout. "How often do these go down in Atlanta, huh? I'm performing one night that I told you about months ago! Then I take off for five other countries! Why the fuck can't you be there?"

"I'm having dinner with the President."

My jaw clamps as I trudge over to the west side of my loft. There's a gorgeous sunset out the iron-framed window, yesterday morning's rain a memory. "Real nice, Elijah. The one excuse I can't argue with. Other than your having dinner with God."

"You want me to cancel?"

With heavy sarcasm, I chuckle, "Yeah do it."

"You know he's not a fan of who I'm working for, and if I can change that he'll help me."

"The President?"

"The Senator. Impress him and he'll have my back. I want to make it there before Dad did. You know that."

"You're still in fucking law school!"

"I'm an overachiever."

Blinking at the view I run a hand through my hair, another reminder of how much we've grown apart as we've gotten older. Mine's much longer than his hair for the first time. Feels like we have nothing in common these days despite being identical twins. When we were growing up we were inseparable. Now I never see him except for holidays or huge events like Ethan or Hannah's weddings. Partly my fault for having this career where I'm touring on the road all the time, but when I'm in town I expect to see him. Especially since he switched universities to be nearer to family.

"I'm here one night, Elijah."

"You grew up in the same house I did. You saw the games! Give me a fucking break. This is politics. It's who you know in Washington *now and in the future,* not the past. It hardly matters that dad and Grandpa were in Washington. I have to claw my way up."

"When you're ready you'll have the people's vote."

"What good will that do me if I don't have the support of the majority in Congress. One Senator at a time I am kissing ass and showing what I can do. Word spreads. I keep moving up with friends on my side, not enemies trying to kill me. Fuck, why am I even arguing about this? You saw what Dad had to do! And you're going to have thousands of people screaming your name. Why do you even need *me* there?"

I almost throw the phone across the room. Through gritted teeth I tell him, "Because you're my best friend, you dick. I'm hanging up now."

Maggie looks up from my blue leather couch as I growl at the dark screen. "If it makes you feel any better, your sister Hannah just tweeted how proud she is of her little brother."

I collapse next to my publicist and steal her cell. "Give me that."

"Hey!" She reaches for it but I easily hold it out of reach while she claws at me. "Gabriel, stop it! I'm nothing without my phone!"

"It's the other way around, Maggie," I smirk, jumping up. She chases me around the loft but I dodge her like a pro. "Had lots of practice with my sister! She's way taller than you are. You're playing a losing game, Mags!"

Growing bored I toss it to her. She doesn't catch it and the thing shatters. "No! You bastard! I just bought that!"

Heading to my fridge I say over my shoulder, "I'll buy you a new one."

Delicately patting down the fragments of her screen as if it'll do anything other than cut her fingers, Maggie follows me. "Why can't he be there?"

"He has a hot date." Off her look I dryly mutter, "And it's a guy." We stare at each other as I pop open an ice-cold beer and take a swig.

"It's the President isn't it?"

"Just drop it."

A mass of dark curls bobble as she shakes her head. "You've got that date coming up, too."

Leaning against my granite counter I hold the bottle to my lips and tell her, "I don't date, Mags, you know that."

"The contest you forgetful piece of fluff."

I snort and feel the burn of beer in the back of my damn nostrils as she grabs her purse to leave. "You made me spit out of my nose. Why do I keep you around when you talk to me like that?"

Gingerly holding her mangled addiction as her purse strap threatens to bend her forearm in half, Maggie reaches for the doorknob. "Because you like the abuse? And no other publicist is as good as I am? Either one works. Your date is this Thursday, that's two days from now. Since I know you won't choose a restaurant on your own or actually show up unless I make you, I've already reserved the best table at Rays on The River, and a car will arrive here at 7:30 P.M sharp to drag you there."

"Will I even be awake by then?" I dryly ask her.

She cocks her head. "Elijah got you in a mood didn't he."

"No shit."

"Try to be nice to the poor girl, bless her innocent fangirl heart."

My shoulders slump as I push off the counter and head for my couch. "You've gotta be fucking kidding me. You didn't set me up with a virgin, did you?"

"Oh my God!" Maggie explodes. "First of all, I'm your publicist, not your pimp! Second, you should be a gentleman and not even care!" We stare at each other until she starts smiling. "Right, there are no gentlemen present, what was I thinking?"

"Unless you look in the mirror, muff-diver."

"I resemble that remark."

"When are you going to let me watch, Mags? You and Carrie scissoring like little kitties in a pile of catnip, I want in." I take a slug of beer as she cracks up. I barely break a smile because I'm too practiced at breaking someone's balls, male or female. You're not a member of my family if you can't take it as good as you get it. Besides, I'm still pissed at Elijah.

"Gabriel!" she groans through laughter. "If I had known working for you would have been like this!"

"You would have begged to work for me when you were still accepting cock for supper?"

Her lips go tight in an effort to maintain severity. It's not working. "You would have been my last man ever. Because trust me, I would have given up the dong after being with a dick like you."

I lazily smirk, "You've never been with a Cocker."

"Every man says that. That's the number one thing lesbians hear from men we don't want to fuck – *if only you had my dick you wouldn't want pussy*. So you're not original. I'll see you later. I'm going to get a replacement for this phone. And I'm putting it on your bill!"

"Never doubted that for a second."

"You need to get laid."

"Got some last night."

Cocking an eyebrow she walks out the door. "You need to get laid *right*." Holding up her hand she shouts, "I get the last word this time!"

Right before it shuts, I mutter, "Word."

She opens it. "I heard that!"

"Word."

Maggie growls and vanishes, which is technically not using actual language.

So I got the last word.

PAIGE

"*I* thought maybe this time you weren't coming back."

Bobby won't meet my eyes as he shrugs his jacket off. "Why wouldn't I come home?"

I shove my hands into the deep pockets of my favorite baggy sweatpants, my loose tank top billowing from the wind as he shuts the front door. "Another storm?"

"Yeah."

I wait for him to say more. It's a fool's hope.

As he kicks off his shoes I ask, "Three days ago I woke up thinking you were at the house-painting job, until he called and asked why you never showed up. What do you want me to do here, Bobby?"

"What do you mean?"

"Oh come on, I'm not dumb. Please look at me."

His guilt stays fixed on the floor as he whispers, "Paige."

I go to him and cup his face in my hands. "What were you thinking?"

Tears liquefy his sweet brown eyes, lashes fluttering with shame. "I was up two thousand and then it was gone."

"It's always gone! Rent is due on Monday and we're already one month behind. Why did you do this to us?"

He holds my hands on his cheeks, voice hoarse, breath reeking of cigarettes. "If I won big I could have paid you back."

Oh my God, you're just like Mom.

Of course it was a noble idea that drove him to take the meager amount of pay he'd saved up and throw it down the pit called a poker table. That's what breaks my heart even more. I covered his rent for the last four months. But my savings has been bled dry now. We had to shut off cable and Wi-Fi already. Electricity bills are bi-monthly so we have a little more time. Not that it will matter when we got evicted. Don't need the lights if nobody is here to turn them on.

We grew up under the shadow of this disease until our mother found Gamblers Anonymous. When he showed signs he had it, too, Mom and Dad held him up for a while. But then they washed their hands of Bobby.

I couldn't do that.

I just couldn't.

When my brother's gambling finally made him homeless, I asked my then-roommate to move out.

I have to take care of my brother.

You're enabling him, Paige! Don't you see he's an addict?

I'm all he has.

But I never wanted to be homeless *with* him.

"Bobby! We could have begged the landlord for a little more time if we had most of this month's rent at least! And you could have asked that contractor if he had more work. But you didn't show up. I begged him to give you another chance and he said no! Why do you keep doing this?"

"I'm so sorry."

I whisper, "I know," staring at the ground.

He covers his beautiful face, groaning through trembling fingers, "I was up two thousand! It was incredible." He drops his hands, glee shining from his eyes. "I wish you could have seen it! I thought my time had come."

Childhood memories sting my eyes as I stare at my brother.

Defeated I ask him, "Are you tired?"

"Exhausted."

"Why don't you get some sleep...?"

He nods and shuffles to his bedroom as I flop onto this stupid old couch and bring my knees to my chest. What am I going to do? Our landlord is the biggest snob, an elitist bastard who inherited six wonderful apartment buildings from his much-kinder father who passed away last winter. Inman Park is too cool a neighborhood to not pay your rent in. He's looking for any reason to get rid of us so he can get new people in here at twice the price. People who can actually pay him. He gave us until Monday and made it clear that he will slam a *Notice To Evict* letter on our door for the world to see if the cash isn't in his insatiable palm by midnight.

We have no place to go. Shelby lives with her boyfriend in a one-bedroom. My boss, Jordanna, has seven cats that would send my allergies to the hospital after one night. I can't live with Mom and Dad again. The dysfunction in that co-dependent household would have me slitting my wrists, especially when I know they'd never let my brother come with me.

"Paige?" Bobby tentatively whispers, afraid to come into the living room.

I lift my head and wipe my eyes. "Yeah?"

"I'm going to get a job. A real one. Not just painting houses for some asshole. I'll pay you back."

The hope in his eyes kills me.

"That'd be great."

He smiles and opens his arms. "I'm so sorry."

Rising to let him fold into me I whisper in his hair. "I'll think of something."

PAIGE

The thing about a cheap phone is my silencing feature died months ago. Groaning, I reach for the nightstand and smack my hand around until I locate the vibrating annoyance. Don't even check who's calling.

Just yank it to my ear and grumble, "Hello?"

In a hushed voice Shelby says, "Tell me you're not sleeping!"

"I'm not anymore!" I sigh, rolling onto my back with my eyes still closed. "I thought your car got fixed. Is it still in the shop?"

"I'm not calling for a ride. It's five minutes to seven and your class is sitting in there on their mats, stretching like you're going to walk in at any minute."

Jackknifing up, I scream, "No! Oh my God!"

"I'm kidding," she dryly says. "No, I'm not! I'm dead

fucking serious. Get your ass down here because I've been telling Jordanna you're on your way."

I shout while yanking yoga pants up my groggy legs, "Of course she picks today to show up and check on us. Oh my God, Shelby! It'll take me at least fifteen minutes to get from here to there!"

My brother cracks the door open while covering his eyes. "Not if you blast through all the reds."

"Bobby! I'm not dressed. Oh, you can't see me. Hang on!" I tug my sports bra into place and grab my mesh tank top and flip-flops. "Okay you can look." Into the phone I tell Shelby, "Bobby is going to drive me and it's not gonna be the legal way!!!"

"Hurry!" she hisses before hanging up.

Bobby and I race through the apartment, bursting out the door without bothering to lock it. "If we get robbed, what are they going to take?" I joke as we nearly crash into old Mr. Parker coming out of his apartment for the morning paper.

"Watch it!"

"Sorry, Mr. P!" Bobby calls over his shoulder. "She's late for work!"

"Oh, it's you two!" he mutters. "Well go on!"

We jump the final steps, land on the pavement and dash for my car, leaping into the Honda with Bobby behind the wheel. He tears out of the parking space leaving tire marks as evidence. I'm gripping the oh-shit-handle, swaying as he whips onto Piedmont slicing in and out of traffic. Honking with his muscles wired tightly he ignores red light after light, shouting out the open windows, "Out of the way! Comin' through!"

Under my breath I give a strained laugh. "This is terrifying, but thank you."

"I'm the reason you slept late." He turns the wheel and narrowly avoids an old truck going forty in a thirty mile-per-hour zone. The guy honks at us. Bobby gives him the finger. More honking ensues and the guy floors it. Now we're in a chase with this asshole practically grazing the right side of my car. The only one we have. I roll my window down to nicely tell the guy I'm late for work, it's not personal.

My brother shouts, "Hey fuckhead! Your mother sucked my cock last night! And she wasn't good!"

"Bobby!" I cry out, head swinging toward him.

I sway as the guy pushes his car into us on purpose.

My old Honda hits the middle divider.

It bounces back into our lane and crashes into the truck.

Both vehicles go spinning right.

Traffic screeches behind us.

Eight other cars hit each other.

Horns explode in the morning air.

I grab the dashboard. "Tell me this isn't happening."

Bobby mutters, "What a fucking asshole."

My mouth drops open as I stare at him. His eyes lock onto something behind me. I turn around and see the truck's door is open and the guy is heading for us, crooking his finger at Bobby to get out and fight. The guy is gorgeous, dressed in faded blue jeans and worn-down boots, so tall I have to crane to look up at him as he gets closer.

There's no way I'm letting him near my brother.

Clawing the door open I leap out. "You could have killed me! You didn't care that there was *a woman* in this seat?"

Emerald green eyes narrow on me as he tilts his head in anger. "I barely nicked you. Cut the drama."

Motioning to the honking cars and police sirens getting louder by the second, I shout, "Oh you mean this drama that you created, you evil giant?!"

Bobby is ready to fight, but he's only five-seven and scrawny, so this match isn't even.

I jump between their male egos. "No! I will not allow this!"

The gorgeous giant says, "Nobody talks about my mother like that, you piece of shit!"

I push him in the chest. "And nobody talks to my brother like that, you big animal!"

Bobby growls, "Paige, stay out of this."

Sirens roar to a deafening level and a horn speaker thingy blasts with the policeman's voice. "Step back and throw your hands up! Everybody on the ground!"

I yank Bobby's arm. "Come on!"

"No fuckin' way."

"You have to make this right. I can't lose my job, get evicted, and get you out of jail in the same week!"

His nostrils flare as he fights his inner demons. He nods and we both go to our knees.

The giant was watching us from the corners of his eyes. He hesitates and joins us.

There are now three police cars at the pileup.

Like he has cantaloupes for balls, the first cop saunters up.

"Ben Cocker, that you?" he asks.

Giant guy smirks at him. "You just want to see me on my knees, don't you, Timothy?"

"Your Senator relative going to bail you out this time, too?"

"You going to call him?"

The cop smirks and motions for us to rise. "Alright, on your feet."

He looks at my brother in a weird way.

My heart is pounding. I'm barely able to focus. I glance over to find Bobby is glaring at the cop.

So I start talking. "Listen, Officer..."

Giant guy cuts me off. "It was *my* fault, Tim. I was texting and didn't realize the wheel veered left. I ran into them. They bounced off the medium. We all turned to avoid each other but we were too close and smashed sides again on the way back. That pileup behind us, they were just trying to get out of the damn way. It was an honest mistake."

The cop eyes him. "Why should I believe a word

you say, Ben? The amount of shit your family gets away with I should take you in just to watch you get out of it. I need the entertainment." He glances to me. "That true what he said?"

"Uh…"

Bobby coughs for attention and answers for me, "Totally true. We were just trying to get my sister to work. She's late for work."

I mutter, with my gaze dropping at the reminder, "Very late and probably fired."

Giant runs a hand through his sandy-brown hair and asks from under his eyebrows, "Why would I lie? You know the fine you're going to slap me with, the ding on my record. Hiked insurance. You really think I'd pay that price to help these guys? Complete strangers?"

I glance over wondering what the hell he's doing.

First he's reacting to my brother cussing by ramming into us, and now he's personally taking the blame? Sure he's lying, but still.

Why the switch?

Officer Tim has a chip on both shoulders where the giant is concerned. They go way back in a bad way. He grumbles, staring into the sun, "Well, I can't take you into the station on an accidental accident."

Bobby and I exchange a look at the redundancy. Just one accident would have been fine. I mean, that's the definition of the word.

Clicking his tongue as he considers what to do,

Officer Timothy finally says, "But I will give you that fine so get ready for an insurance premium hike that will wipe that fuckin' smirk right off your face, Ben!" He heads back to his car. "You just wait right there!"

"I'm fired. This is it. No job. No house. Nothing."

"It's my fault," Bobby groans, under his breath. "If I hadn't gambled that money away."

"Just stop it. What's done is done." I grab his hand and turn to look down the street. "We're so close though. I can't believe this."

Bobby calls to the cop. "Can we leave? I think the car still runs. I need to get her to *Om This Yoga*, and it's only three blocks up."

Officer Tim shakes his head, slowly reaching into his car for the pad of tickets.

"Fuckin' prick," Bobby mutters.

Giant mutters back, "Just hang tight. It'll only get worse if you fight this guy, trust me."

I glance between them. "Now you get along!?"

It takes an eternity to give our information. He stops writing twice and saunters off to the other policemen as they write down first hand accounts from the pile-up people. He does this on purpose, just to mess with this Ben guy, which makes me want to tear the cop's smug mustache right off.

After we've finally been dismissed to my newly dented car, Officer Timothy yells, "No speeding now! I will pull you over!"

Turning on the ignition Bobby mutters to me, "Let me hit him."

Ignoring him I lock eyes with our assailant.

As he goes to get in his truck, Ben tips his head like he's got a cowboy hat on. He doesn't.

I point at him and mouth, "This is your fault."

*B*obby reaches over to comfort me as we pull into the parking lot. "Hey, don't! She won't fire you."

"Yes she will! She doesn't have an evolved or forgiving bone in her body, despite how she presents herself."

"Ironic for a woman who owns a yoga studio."

"Right? She barely even practices! She's a trust fund baby who bought *Om This* to make her feel important around her rich friends, took the Teachers Training to give her facade credibility. If she taught my class she will be pissed *I* made her look bad. She will fire me the second she gets me alone."

My eyes widen as I spot my Thursday morning die-hards filing out of the front door. Ducking down I cover my head and decide a second later not to be such a wuss. "Oh fuck it. Why am I hiding? Let me out."

"I'm almost there. Just hang on."

"Stop the car!" He slows and I jump out while it's still moving.

This could be graceful and superhero-esque if I had any luck today.

I don't.

Instead I go rolling and scrape up my right arm. "Ouch!"

Some of the my students run over, Laura yelling her concern the loudest. "Oh my God, Paige! Are you okay?!"

Climbing up with the help of Najma's offered hand, I limp toward the studio. "I'm so sorry I missed class."

Najma mutters a tentative, "It wasn't the same, that's for sure," as she walks with me and Laura back to *Om This.*

Others who saw my tumble join us.

Ashley jogs up, joking, "Why jump out of a perfectly good vehicle?"

Dee Dee asks with concern, "You okay?"

"I don't know. Walk with me, okay?"

"Of course!"

Jodi runs up for the left side and winces at my arm. "Oh, honey, you need to wash that out soon!"

And though she was almost to her car, Susi — who has been to every Thursday class I've ever had — rushes back to see why I wasn't here. "Class was awful! Where were you? Are you sick?"

Laura points to my car, now parked with Bobby waiting for the verdict. "Paige, is that your boyfriend?"

"If he was my boyfriend, I would have broken up with him by now. He's my brother."

He and I lock eyes as I walk inside *Om This* where the two Lindas are talking to Shelby. They're best friends who always introduce themselves by saying, 'Yes, we're both named Linda. You'll get used to it.'

Linda N. glances over at our entrance, takes one look at me and says, "What the fuck happened to you?"

Linda M. mutters, "Only *you* would cuss before nine in the morning."

"Is there a schedule on cussing? If so, clock me in."

Shelby comes forward with a single glance over to Studio 1. "Jordanna's in there." To everyone else she says, "You guys go with her."

Beth comes out of the bathroom with her phone to her ear, "No, I just changed and I'll be at the office in two shakes of a lamb's...what the hell? I'll call you back." She joins the march.

Jordanna Stevens is stacking bolsters with her usual amount of sloppiness. Her long black hair is pinned up like a geisha's and her outfit flows as she moves. As she spots us her lips tighten and her blue eyes dart around. She's trying to decide how to handle this.

"Well, Paige, you look...tired."

"She just fell out of a car!" Susi announces while others back up the claim and murmur concern. Those who did *not* see my stunt, give each other looks.

Words won't come out of my mouth, I'm so anxious. I can see behind her eyes that she is furious I've put her in a position where she cannot tell me what she really thinks.

She clears her throat and blinks too many times. "So, you fell out of a moving vehicle and missed class. Well, that's…normal. I mean, *acceptable.* As an excuse not to be here."

Awkward.

I try to speak but still…nothing.

She brightens and adds, "And I had such a wonderful time teaching you all. It was a gift in disguise. Not your arm getting hurt. You know what I mean."

Weakly I nod, waiting for her to lose her mind as soon as they all leave.

Beth's phone rings. "Oh, I have to go to work. I was just dying of curiosity, but Paige, you're okay?"

"Uh huh."

Everyone except Shelby says goodbye, some reaching for my hand and giving it a squeeze. Linda M. even gives me a hug. "Call if you need me?"

"Promise."

The room empties leaving only Shelby and me with the predictably two-faced Jordanna Stevens. Her head tilts and she crosses her arms. "I can't wait to hear this, because that car couldn't have been moving very fast to create those little scratches."

My lips part, but a male voice echoes off the walls instead of mine. "I ran into her car back on Piedmont."

Jordanna and I look over.

"Ben Cocker," he smiles extending his hand, and damn if he isn't more handsome with those white teeth shining on us.

Shelby and I exchange a look.

That's when it hits me for the first time. "Wait, Ben *Cocker*?"

Shelby tries her best to appear cool. "Like related to *Gabriel Cocker*, Ben Cocker?"

"He's my cousin, yeah." On a glance back to Jordanna he says, "But I'm way better looking than him in person."

She giggles. "I'm Jordanna Stevens. So nice to meet you, Ben."

Running a steady hand through his thick, sandy hair, he throws her a sexy smile like cupid's arrow just hit him.

They're perfect for each other.

She's a nightmare and he runs strangers off the road. Great match!

I start backing away. "Gonna go clean this arm up."

He didn't hear me.

Neither did she.

Ben's voice is deeper than before as he asks her, "So uh…you have a partner, or is this all yours?"

Jordanna gazes up at him. "It's just me."

"Impressive."

"You think so? I mean, it's hard work running your own business but it's so fulfilling, you know?"

Shelby and I almost gag. As soon as we're out of the room she whispers, "*We* run this place! You even do the damn bookkeeping!"

"I know!" Outside I see Bobby waiting on the sidewalk with his hands wringing. I hurry out to tell him what happened, and Shelby follows.

Bobby keeps his voice low but he is clearly freaked.

"He said he was going to help, but if he fucked things up even more then I am going to kick his ass, I don't care how tall he is!"

"It's okay! She's flirting with him! She's totally forgotten about me!"

My brother and I fill Shelby in on the car accident, the police officer, and Ben taking the blame.

"You said you weren't lucky, Paige, but it sounds to me like you're the luckiest person alive."

Bobby and I look at each other.

She has no idea about our lack of rent money.

Recounting the ways she thinks I lucked out, she finishes with, "And you have that date with Gabriel Cocker tonight!"

Like I've been slapped I take a step back. "I forgot about it! But I can't go!"

"What do you mean you *can't go?*" she demands.

Bobby mutters, "You have a date with who? Wait, what the fuck? The rockstar Gabriel??"

Shelby blinks, confused. "How come Bobby doesn't know?"

Staring at her I struggle to answer that question. I can't tell her it's because he didn't come home for three days and my life is a mess. This dinner date that any other girl would die for is the last way I want to spend my time. I need to find a way to make money and make it fast. I'm running on three hours of sleep and I have four classes left to teach today. Those are still not enough and never would be. Yoga teachers don't exactly rake in the dough. That's not why we get into this field.

I exhale and firmly say, "Because I'm not going, that's why I didn't tell Bobby."

Shelby's jaw drops

I turn on my heel and walk inside, right into Ben. He flashes Jordanna's business card that has a heart hand-drawn on it, and mutters, "Outside."

Frowning I hesitate and follow him.

As soon as the door closes the four of us make a circle, with Bobby constantly shuffling his feet.

"That woman is crazy," Ben quietly says.

Shelby rolls her eyes. "Duh. Thank God you saw it because I was about to warn you."

I blurt, "Wait…you were *faking* interest?"

He shrugs. "She was going to fire you. It distracted her."

He's looking at me in a disarming way, and then determination flashes over his dark green eyes.

"Why are you looking at me like that?"

He takes my good arm and pulls me from view of the windows. "Go out with me, Paige."

Bobby explodes with anger. "No fuckin' way! You're a psycho!"

"I'm not going out with you!"

He smirks from Bobby to me, "I'm not a psycho. I just have a lot of insurance and I was in a bad mood this morning for reasons I'm not going into right now." He shifts his intense gaze back to me to explain why he wants to date me, "When you stood up for your brother that was amazing…"

Shelby interrupts him, "Excuse me." She stands between us, craning her neck. "You're clearly used to getting your way with these handsome looks of yours and this slammin' body, but you ran into my best friend here so not only are her brother and I not allowing you to keep talking nonsense but she's already got a date tonight…with your cousin Gabriel!" Over her shoulder she cocks her eyebrow at me. "See what I mean? Luckiest girl alive." She swings back to him. "I however am available."

Bobby mutters, "I thought you live with your boyfriend."

Shelby says, "Shhh!"

But Ben's locked on me, confused. "When did you guys start dating? I didn't know Gabriel was seeing anyone, and he hasn't been in Atlanta for months."

Shelby sucks on her lips.

I do the same.

Bobby is glaring at him.

Ben looks around. "Why is nobody talking?"

On a reluctant breath I confess, "I won a date with him. We've never met. It was a radio contest. But I wouldn't go out with you anyway. Because you are indeed a psycho."

He smiles his charismatic smile, eyes glittering with amusement. "If anyone in my family heard you call me that, they'd think you were the crazy one."

"You ran into our car!" I cry out.

In a low, steady voice Ben says, "He said my mother sucked...well, I won't repeat it. But nobody talks about my mom like that. I needed to get him out of the car so I could kick his ass. I'm just like you. I look out for my own. Plus I have a temper. It runs in the family so get ready when you meet my cousin tonight." He turns on his worn boot heel and heads off, his perfect ass ticking slowly as he runs a hand through his sun-kissed hair. Over his shoulder he locks eyes with me and asks, "Where are you two going tonight?"

"I'm not telling you!"

Laughing, Ben jumps in his old beat-up truck and pulls away like he's got nothing but time. Bobby, Shelby and I stare like we've got nothing but shock.

"Where *is* Gabriel taking you?" Shelby asks.

"Who knows," I mutter. "I've been kind of busy."

GABRIEL

There are a couple half-eaten sandwiches on Ethan's fully stocked bar that are waiting for my mouth. He thinks one of those is his but he's mistaken. Since his pregnant fiancé keeps interrupting our pool game with texts and phone calls, I've taken it upon myself to enjoy both the roast beef with swiss cheese *and* the turkey with avocado. He won't notice until they're gone. Not my problem.

Gauging where the cue ball is in geometric relation to the green number six ball I bend over, slide the pool stick back and forth over the slope between my index and middle knuckles, and aim. I pull back and take the shot. I relish the cracking sound, nothing like it. There's something old school about this game that makes a man feel like a man. And since I made that corner pocket as I intended to, it's time for chowing down.

"Highness, I know you want the baby out of you now. It's almost time. Hang in there."

I snort under my breath and vow never to be in his shoes. Sure they're in love, whatever, I just don't see myself ever settling down. With all the ass I get touring, why would I want to block the river of pussy flowing my way? No man would willingly do something that fucking stupid.

"Princess, stop swearing. Our daughter can hear you from the womb, and I want her to be a lady." He locks eyes with me and grins on a wink. He doesn't even see me stuffing this roast beef in my mouth. It's the one he wanted most.

Love.

It blinds you.

"Okay, look," he continues, heading off while rubbing the back of his head. He's dressed in jeans and a graphic T-shirt, with sneakers kicked off and holes in his socks. I stare at them and open my mouth wide enough to shove an even bigger bite down my gullet before he catches on.

"I'm sending a foot masseuse over there to rub your feet right after this lunch meeting with Albert Fucking Cosnick. I'll even tell Dolores she's coming." Ethan pauses and leans on the arched doorway, facing away from the game room. I polish off the rest of his sandwich as he says, "Yes, the masseuse will be female. And no I'm not fucking her."

I almost choke from laughter. He'd told me Charlie

has gotten weird in the final pregnancy stage. Jealous as hell. He thinks it's adorable.

"Highness, I'm not sending a dude to rub my wife's feet, so breathe deeply. You're panting."

I go take another shot and miss this time.

My mouth is as full as a squirrel hoarding his whole winter stash.

"Yes, I know you didn't realize it was going to be this hard. But you know what Hannah said. When our little Kaya is in your arms you will forget all about these mood swings and beg me to impregnate you again. Who is that talking in the background? Are you calling me in the middle of your meeting? Go take care of your corporation, you nut. I love you. You sure you can't shorten the day and come home early?"

I explode, "Oh, come on, give me a fuckin' break over here! It's your turn!"

He waves at me without looking back, saying into the phone, "If you decide to leave work early give me a call. I'll kick Gabriel out of the mansion and show you what a real massage is."

The turkey and avocado is in my hands now and I can't open my mouth any wider than this. Half is devoured before he hangs up and walks to his pool cue. "What am I again? Stripes or solids?"

"Stripes. You make me ill with all that gooshy crap, Ethan. Pussy, meet whipped. And you're the pussy."

Lazily chuckling, "I won't deny it," my cousin gauges the eleven ball. It glides into the side pocket with a bank shot. "Who's the best pool player in the world!? I am. That's right. Me!" He looks over to the empty plates. "What the fuck!?"

I swallow down the last chuck of deliciousness. "What? Missing something?"

"You ate my lunch! That I made for you!"

"I thought it was all for me."

"You'll never change, will you?"

"Don't see any reason to."

He glares at me. "Remember that time you took the last deviled egg at the BBQ?"

"Which time?"

Growling he aims at the green-striped fourteen ball, takes the shot and misses, accidentally knocking the eight ball into the corner pocket and losing the game.

"I thought you were the best pool player in the world? Oh right, that's me."

He tosses his stick on the table and grumbles, "When are you leaving town again?"

My phone rings and I pull it out of my black jeans, chuckling, "You love me, don't act like you don't." As I answer the phone I ask him one final, disgusting question. "You want the sandwiches back? I could stick my finger down my…hello?"

Maggie sounds impatient, but that's her normal way of speaking. "You haven't texted me back. Confirm the restaurant so I know you'll be there."

"What do I care where we're going if the driver is taking us there?"

She pauses at my logic. During that beat a call comes through from my cousin. I put her on hold without telling her, and say, "Yo, Ben. I'm here at Ethan's and I just kicked his ass in pool."

Ethan shouts, "I got the eight ball in! He didn't beat me!"

I put it on speaker and tell Ben, "That's still losing."

He responds, "Yeah, he still lost."

"It's not really losing!" Ethan argues.

Ben and I both say at the same time as I hold the phone up, "Yeah it fuckin' is."

"Whatever."

Ben's voice changes to overly casual as he asks, "Hey, uh, Gabriel. I heard someone won a date with you on a radio station."

Taking it off speaker I hold up my finger out to Ethan and say, "Don't even start!" He rushes me, grabs the phone before I can react quickly enough.

Ethan chortles while putting the phone back on fucking speaker, "What's this? Someone thinks going out with Gabriel is a prize? Has she met him?"

Ben seems distracted though, because he doesn't join in on the hazing. "Gabriel, you still there?"

"Yes. Why. Hurry this up. It's ridiculous and I don't wanna talk about it."

There's a long pause to the point where we think the call got dropped. Finally Ben's voice comes through, again overly casual. "Where you going?"

"To Rays on The River – why?"

"I was just *curious* where something like this would go down. You meet her yet?"

"No."

"See her?"

"No, I've never seen her. Why are you asking?"

I can almost hear him shrug as he says, "You know. Just curious."

Ethan and I are staring at each other.

He has no clue why Ben's acting so weird, either.

Slowly I say, "You said you were curious twice. What's up?"

"I've got another call coming through. Catch you guys later." Ben hangs up.

Ethan mutters, "What the fuck was that about?"

"I have no idea. Oh shit!" Grabbing the phone I take Maggie off hold. "You still there?"

"I want a raise."

"*H*e's gotta be loaded," my brother says while I'm sliding on nude strappy heels. "Wear something tighter."

"Bobby!" I snap, glaring at him with a look that tells him I'm not whoring myself out for rent money.

"I'm kidding!" he laughs.

Shelby shrugs, "I would wear something sexier, Paige," as I walk to the mirror hanging from my wall.

It's a little warped like a mild version of one of those carnival mirrors. I can never see what I really look like. I think this thing is wearing down my confidence. Maybe they're right. Should I put something more alluring on? This lavender dress isn't overtly sexy but I think it's pretty, and classy. The skirt flows, the sleeves are short and the V-neck isn't low.

From my bed she eyes me and shakes her head. "Wear the red mini-dress. You can still rock those nude heels, Paige. But give the guy something to work with here."

"I have no intention of sleeping with him, so I don't want to give him the wrong impression. And look at my arm!" Inspecting the road rash in the mirror I ask my best friend, "Did the gauze really look that bad?"

She and Bobby both shout, "Yes!"

"God, you guys! Have I really asked that many times?"

Shelby sighs, "You look like a hospital victim with gauze. This way it's almost cool, like a tattoo. A red one." Under her breath she says, "The one single girl in Atlanta who doesn't want to sleep with Gabriel and she's the one who wins."

"You won, not me. You're the one who called in! Why don't you dump Carter and go out with Gabriel yourself? What time is it?" We all look at my blinking alarm clock. "Now I know why I didn't wake up. There must have been a power outage with that storm last night."

Shelby frowns, trying to recall one. "It wasn't raining when I went to bed at midnight."

Bobby and I exchange a quick look. He covers for us, "It was late. Woke us up around three or something. Isn't that right?"

Nodding I glance back to the funky mirror and close my eyes, the knot in my stomach tightening. I hate lying to her, but I can't have another person dragged into the drama of my brother's addiction. If I lost Shelby like I did the friendship with my old room-mate, it would be like losing a sister. I'm not willing to risk it.

She digs her phone from her purse, drops it and freaks out. "He'll be knocking any minute!"

"Oh God!" I groan. "Just pose as me and you go!"

She snatches my clutch bag from the dresser and shoves me out of the room. Bobby steps back to make way for us, flattening himself along the wall.

"Here's what we're going to do. You'll go downstairs now and wait outside while I take pictures from the roof. Bobby, grab my purse from the bed! And make sure you get my phone, too."

"Done!" he calls out, disappearing.

"Shelbs, I don't feel good."

"It's like two hours max and you're going to spend it sitting across from a god while eating a delicious meal you don't have to pay for. You can do this! It's not life altering. It's just dinner!" Shoving me out the front door she mutters, "That accident really messed with your head."

"Yeah," I whisper, standing on the doormat staring at her like she might rescue me.

It's the nearing eviction not the accident, Shelby. I wish I could tell you that!

Her arm flies out, index finger stretched to full length. "Go!"

Shuffling to the elevator I push the button. Her

head is poked into our building's hallway. "That thing takes forever! Stop stalling. Take the stairs."

"You take the stairs. These are four inch heels!"

"Oh, right." Her severe expression softens into joy as Bobby hands her purse to her. "Oh my God, you're about to meet Gabriel Cocker! I'm going to take so many pictures! Tell him I'm crazy about his music! *Existence* is my favorite! Ask him why he doesn't do country!"

The elevator opens and I walk inside as they head toward the stairs. "You need to let that go," I call after her.

"Never!" she shouts, and in a lower, excited register says, "Hurry, Bobby! I want to get the perfect shot!"

GABRIEL

I mutter to myself, "Inman Park huh? Nice," as the driver takes me by one of those neighborhood-welcoming murals that are all over Atlanta.

This vehicle is a little overdone for my taste. Booking this obnoxious ride was Maggie's handiwork, probably to impress the contest winner.

I get driven around all the time.

But a fucking *stretch* limo?

What is this…Prom?

The car slows in front of a modern apartment building. Out of boredom I check social media and click *like* on a couple photos that scroll lazily by. I look up as the driver jumps out of the car to come open my door.

Fuck that shit.

I climb out and wave him down. "I can get my own door. It's cool."

He looks at something behind me, and reacts.

Turning around I discover a beautiful, heart-shaped-faced brunette staring at me, biting her bottom lip. My eyes narrow as I feel a punch against my chest.

"Paige Miller?"

"Uh huh," she frowns.

She's not dressed how my groupies usually do when trying to catch my eye, and somehow that is shockingly hot to me. She's stunning in a simple, light purple dress with heels that match her skin and make her legs look chewable. On her wrist is a thin, gold bracelet. There's a tattoo on her right ankle I can't quite see from here. Subconsciously I lick my lips as I walk to introduce myself and get a look at that ankle.

She takes a step back.

I pause and cock my head. "I'm not going to bite you," I smirk.

Her voice is soft and quiet. "I know."

"Unless you want me to." Off her frown I say, "I'm kidding! Trying to make you smile." I soak in her features. There's something really vulnerable about her. Hurt. Guarded. Suddenly it occurs to me that she's probably scared to death about meeting me in person.

"I'm Gabriel, by the way."

"I know who you are."

"Right. Sorry." God, why am I feeling weird? Is this what awkward feels like? I know how to act around women. But my tongue is tied. Running my hand through my hair I ask, "You ready to go?"

Paige is staring at me like she's about to run. "Sure."

A step closer I lean in.

She doesn't pull back, just returns my curious gaze. That's interesting. So it's not fear I saw, there's something else going on.

"Wow," I whisper, drinking her in.

Paige's voice is barely audible as she asks, "What?"

"You're beautiful."

Her deep brown eyes become even larger, long eyelashes fluttering in surprise. She bites her lip again and I look at it, which makes her look at mine. We lock eyes again and I swear to God I almost kiss the girl. I'm stepping back when I decide, fuck it. Gently cupping her chin I lift her lips to mine and press a kiss onto them. Tingles shoot down my entire body, which has never happened. I don't move. She doesn't either. We both pull away at the same time.

Laying my hand on her lower back I lead her to the car and motion to the driver that I'll help her in. He strolls to the front seat as Paige and I look at each other. Our eyes remain locked as she slides her fingers onto my palm and gracefully lowers herself onto the seat. When she releases my hand I feel the absence and as she looks down to adjust her dress my head shakes like my brain is trying to remember who I am.

Cutting a quick glance to the sky I mutter, "Fuck you. I'm not ready for this yet."

Paige asks, "What?"

"Nothing." I swoop inside, reach for the door handle and shut it with finality.

This night isn't what I thought it was going to be.

PAIGE

*D*ressed in all black with a sexy wooden cross necklace, Gabriel Cocker is every inch the rockstar I expected. He was on the cover of Vanity Fair two months ago when his sweet ballad launched his album all the way to number one on both the Indie Rock and Pop charts. The photograph was panty-melting — him shirtless in only leather pants and this necklace he's wearing now. It was an homage to a photo of a singer from the 1960's or 1970's named Jim Morrison, except that in Gabriel's photo they'd sprayed him down so he was glistening.

But in person Gabriel is every bit as full of himself as I imagined he would be.

Kissing me like that and saying I'm beautiful as if he meant any of it.

Puh-lease.

He's as good an actor as he is a singer, but I'm not fooled.

"You still in college?" he asks, legs spread with total confidence.

Staring ahead I answer, "No."

"What do you do?"

"I'm a yoga teacher."

"Is that how you got this?" He reaches over to glide his fingertips along the soft underbelly of my arm just below my exposed wound. The sensual touch tickles and sends a shiver into parts of me that were sleeping.

My eyelashes rise and I stare at him.

His lips…I can still feel them.

That was a dirty trick he played.

Bringing my arm closer to me I mumble, "This is from a car accident. You didn't hear about it?"

He cocks his head, long strands of black hair hanging free over his perfect forehead. "No, did you tell my publicist about it or something? She didn't say anything."

"Your cousin hit me on the way to work."

Gabriel's blinks in sexy confusion. I swear he could sniff his armpit and it would be hot. "Which one?"

"Ben. Why? How many do you have?"

His jaw grinds as anger flashes across his gorgeous face. He glares out the window and starts tapping the armrest, fingers growing more agitated. This is the first time I've spotted the black leather rope around his right wrist. Something about a man in masculine jewelry makes me think of vikings or gladiators. Either are enough to make my belly warm.

"Sneaky motherfucker," he mutters.

"Sorry?"

He glances back to me and holds. Leaning over so quickly I have no time to react he tries to kiss me again, his fingers wrapping around my head. I push him off and put distance between us as I cry out, "Stop it! What are you doing?"

Those pouty lips of his make an O and he leans way back, staring ahead. "I uh, wow, sorry. Don't know what came over me." Under his breath he groans, "Shit."

"You swear a lot. From your music I wouldn't think you'd do that."

He locks eyes with me and starts ironically laughing. "Listen, *Namaste Chick,* you know nothing about me. I'm not the good guy you think I am."

"Who said I thought you were good?"

"You just did. From my lyrics you think I'm a pussy."

"Swearing doesn't make you a man."

"Wow," he mutters.

"It doesn't. And your songs are beautiful. That doesn't make you a pussy if you write poetry. I just thought…"

"So you're a prude. I'm on a date with a girl who won't say the words shit, fuck, damn, cock. Wait, do you say hell or do you think that's a swearword, too?"

"I think you're an arrogant and conceited jerk, that's what I think! And Namaste is a term of respect so that's not an insult, Gabriel Cocker!"

He glares at me, a million expressions crossing over his face as he tries to figure out what to make of me. "I was wrong."

"About?!"

He sneers, "This night is going to be *exactly* how I thought it would be." Swiping lint off his stylish, black blazer he adds in a lower, bored voice, "A fucking pain in my ass."

"That makes two of us who think this was a terrible idea. I don't want to be here!"

He chuckles while raking that fantastic hair of his, "No shit! I'm pretty clear on that now. Got it. Why don't we just take you home." He leans forward and growls, "Unbelievable."

I look out the windows, too, searching for what he sees. We're driving up to the restaurant. "We can still turn back around."

"Oh no, we're going in. I can't wait to see this." Gabriel swings the door open before the limo comes to a complete stop. He jumps out while the car is still moving except when he does it it's smooth and super-heroesque.

Rolling my eyes I shoot over to get out, legs dangling as the driver chooses the perfect place to park. "Just stop the car!" His eyes meet mine in the rearview and he hits the brakes. Rocking in my seat I mutter to myself, "What a nightmare."

Gabriel does not help me out of the car and when I stand up I see him walking to his cousin Ben, nearly shouting, "Well, what a surprise! Didn't expect you here! Oh wait, yeah I fuckin' did. Come on! Let's eat!"

Ben locks eyes with me as Gabriel walks on ahead of us without looking back. His furious swagger says he's committed to making this the worst evening of my life.

Staring after him I tell Ben, "Your cousin is worse than you!"

He offers me a sexy smirk. "Way worse. Lucky I showed up, huh? You look very nice tonight, Paige."

GABRIEL

The paparazzi attack me the second I walk inside. The bastards tricked me. Usually they're waiting in the bushes. With how small cameras have gotten they can sneak into a fine dining restaurant like this one and the management won't notice.

I back up as men and women who were posing as customers in the bar all start calling my name to get me to look into their lens. Hannah described it once as the sounds of seagulls when you're hung-over, and she nailed it.

Problem is I know Maggie set photos up on purpose since this contest is a publicity stunt after all, and here I am without my date.

"Hey," I smirk, waving slightly as I back pedal and explode out the door, running into Paige and my double-crossing cousin. "Ben, go home." I grab Ms.

Miller's arm and roughly guide her inside, saying under my breath, "Smile."

"No!" she hisses at me. Her eyes widen at the onslaught of cameras and suddenly her teeth are showing.

She's hating every second, same as I am.

Here I thought something had happened between us but boy was I wrong. I look over my shoulder and see Ben peering through the window with his hands in his pockets, trademark family gesture for being unhappy about a situation. Well, he can have her once this night is over. The night before my Atlanta concert I'm not letting it leak that the contest winner hates me. No fucking way. This is my city. I'm not giving it up just because this chick's in a bad mood.

We pose for photos and I give the charming smile I inherited from Dad, "Isn't she beautiful? I lucked out, huh?"

They nod saying various affirmatives, and the cameras keep clicking until one yells out, "Give her a kiss for Creative Loafing, Gabriel!"

Paige starts to object but I swoop in, dip her really low and whisper, "If you play along I'll owe you one."

Her eyes are locked with mine and her arms slide around my neck. We kiss and it happens all over again, that crazy sensation I felt the first time. Only this time she really goes for it, slipping her tongue into my mouth. We rise up, lip-locked, making out for the

Press. And it is fucking hot, this kiss. So smokin' that my cock reacts like we're alone. And we're not.

I pull away and slide my blazer off, leaving only my black T-shirt on so I can hide this erection before it goes viral on the web.

"Okay, we're hungry."

"We saw!" one of the guys jokes.

Everyone laughs.

I stare at him a second.

"Ha ha!" I call out, nodding that he's a funny guy as I lead Paige through the throng. "See you guys tomorrow."

"We'll be there!"

Nodding to the hostess that we're ready for our table, Paige and I follow the woman to an intimate, tucked away booth.

I'm subconsciously licking my lips as my reluctant date slides in. She wipes her mouth.

Under my breath I make a scoffing noise and flop down next to her. "You gotta be kiddin' me."

What a fucking nightmare this shit is.

"What?" she demands.

As if she doesn't know.

"You wiped my kiss off. You know how many women would...fuck it. Never mind. Just look at the menu and tell me what you want to order."

"I can order for myself."

Rolling my eyes I mutter, "Fine. And here I thought

you were just being Southern, but forgive me. I'll be sure to lose my manners."

Under her breath and just as annoyed as I am, she says, "Oh you can't open the door to the restaurant or wait for me to get out of the limo but you'll order my dinner for me. You're a gentleman only when you have an audience."

Glaring at her I shoot back, "You're a complete bitch!"

She slaps my face. Hard. Not a tiny little oh-stop-it-jerk, but one that leaves a mark. I wince and rub the spot as two paparazzi fuckheads jump out, snapping photos. "Did you get that?" One asks the other.

"No, you?"

"Yeah! Ha!"

"Lucky!"

Paige and I are staring at the guys, and they don't even acknowledge we're human and can hear everything they're saying, until I shout, "Get the fuck out of here!"

They jump a little, surprised.

I stand up in the booth and nearly topple our table. "You heard what I said? Get the fuck out of here!"

They start snapping photos.

The manager rushes over. "I'm so sorry, Mr. Cocker. We never invite the media here. We're very discreet with our celebrities. We already asked the others to leave. I didn't know any had snuck by."

"That's worked out real well," I growl, heading for the guy on the right who captured the slap.

Paige leaps up and grabs my wrist. "No, don't! Let's just eat!"

"First let me get that…" I lunge as he's leaving and snatch his camera from him, throwing it to the ground and stepping on it multiple times with all of my strength. "Camera," I finish with a smirk.

Ben strolls up in his nicest jeans, boots, and button-up shirt — like he's going to a wedding or something — and he's holding the other squirming photographer by the collar. "Lose this?"

"Oh Jeezus!" I laugh despite myself. "You're not giving up, are you? Yeah, give me that."

He tosses the paparazzi guy at me and I snatch his camera too. "No!" he grunts, but Ben grabs and throws him backward. I kick the first one with the bottom of my shoe, pushing him. Not too hard where I break anything. Just hurrying his exit.

They take off, one yelling, "I'm going to sue you!"

"I don't fuckin' care, you leech! Be damn sure your record is clean before you come after me!"

The restaurant is silent.

Everyone's watching.

Paige has never seen anything like this.

But Ben and I do this shit all the time. Only difference is never has a girl come between us. The fact that he stuck around after I left him in the parking lot, tells me he's serious about wanting her.

And I don't like that at all.

The manager apologies and asks, "Can I offer you a bottle of wine on the house?"

Ben and I are staring at each other because he's wondering if he should leave or take a seat.

Locked on Ben I tell the manager, "Couple of your best local beers and whatever the unhappy lady is having," letting him know I'm not kicking him out but he'd better watch himself.

The three of us glance to Paige for her order. Her pretty eyes flit from my face to Ben's and back. "I need a shot of tequila."

"Oh shit," chuckles Ben.

I clap him on the shoulder and tell the manager, "Make it three."

PAIGE

It feels like these two are competing for my attention. Gabriel doesn't even like me. Ben hit me with his truck on purpose. These are a couple of way too good-looking, bizarre guys with ulterior motives that make no sense to me, but then again...I'm a little drunk now.

Ben is on my left and Gabriel on my right. They're laughing and one-upping each other with stories from their childhood, and I keep finding myself gazing at Gabriel more.

He has kaleidoscope eyes with an amber streak in one. Other than that little splash, they're the palest of greens on the inside, lighter than I've seen on anyone, and the irises are lined with forest green. When he laughs they catch fire.

"I rode a motorcycle before you," Gabriel smirks, using his freshly refilled shot glass as a pointer.

Ben chuckles, his body relaxed, his shot glass held against his lips. "That's because I had a quad at the ranch. You can't ride a fucking street bike on three hundred acres of unpaved land."

"Half that acreage was cut into by that pansy-ass retreat before you were born! How 'bout you cut that number to its rightful size?"

"It's huge and you know it."

"Not as big as mine."

They're smirking at each other like they could either fight or start cracking up. Tension is thick. Takes me a second to realize they're not talking about land anymore. They're literally comparing penis size, so I cough and speak up for the first time in ten minutes. "I hosted a retreat in Costa Rica once. They're so great for the soul. What kind do you have there?"

Ben's eyebrows rise up a little as he looks at me. "It's changed over the years. We've done yoga, vegan living, even Ayahuasca."

My shot is on the table, finger toying with its rim. "I teach yoga."

Ben smiles, "I know. I was at your studio, remember?"

I laugh, "Oh yeah," my stomach warmed by booze and a delicious meal.

Gabriel's not amused though. He sets his glass down and leans forward. "When were you at her studio?"

I ask Ben, "What is Ayahuasca? I've heard the name. Jordanna mentioned it once. Isn't it illegal?"

"No, it's a healing ritual that a shaman guides you through where you drink a tea and—"

Gabriel cuts him off, "And everyone sits in a tent, pukes into these buckets and hallucinates. It's fucking gross."

I make a face. "They vomit?"

Ben shrugs, "You're detoxing. It's removing everything you're holding onto so you can see your truth."

"What a load of crap," Gabriel mutters.

Tracing the rim of my tiny glass with my fingertip, I look at the raven-haired singer and argue, "I think drugs are a path to the spiritual plane. The one we'll return to once we leave here. I think that's why some people become addicted, because they're touching base with the truth of all things – love. The only problem is that all of us are here for a reason, to learn and grow and negotiate a path for ourselves despite all that life throws at us, to define who we are and finish the contract we made before we were born. We're not supposed to live in the spiritual plane in our human forms. If we visit too often we start to die. That's why addicts look like corpses after a while, they're surfing both worlds and their bodies can't survive it." I pause and bring the glass to my lips on a shrug, "But if you can visit for a little while and not get sucked in, you might gain clarity toward your purpose. It's a danger-ously thin tightrope only some can walk without falling."

Gabriel is staring at me with such intensity that a warmth washes over me as I look at him, my drunken speech over and me sitting here realizing I just rambled a little too much. I glance to Ben and see he's looking at me in exactly the same way.

"I don't know why I said all that."

Gabriel says, "Makes sense to me."

Ben holds his glass out. "Let's drink to spiritual tightropes."

We bring our glasses together and the sound feels like a tear ripping something apart.

Our waiter approaches with the dessert menu. "Can I bring you coffee?"

"Another round," Ben tells him.

Gabriel nods.

I shake my head. "I can't. I feel woozy."

"Only two then," Gabriel tells him, reaching for my hand that's resting on the table.

I glance to Ben whose tense gaze has dropped to our entwining fingers.

I've got to get out of here. Letting go of Gabriel's fingers I announce a little too loudly, "I have to make a phone call!"

Ben climbs out first. Gabriel glares at him as Ben offers his hand to help me stand.

I take it and croak, "Thank you."

His eyes are saying all kinds of sexual things as he smirks, "Anytime."

Oh.

My.

God.

As soon as I'm in the only place where those two men cannot go, I dig my phone out and call Shelby. She doesn't answer at first and I tap my foot on the ladies room tile, heart racing and vision skewed by alcohol.

"How'd it go?"

"Shelbs! Thank God! I thought you had your ringer off or something!"

She tells her boyfriend, "Hit pause, Carter." Coming

back to me, she explains, "We're watching a movie so I didn't hear it vibrate at first. I saw Gabriel kiss you! You're going to die when you see the photo. I'll send it after we get off the phone. Tell me everything!" Her boyfriend groans loudly. "Tell me everything in summary form!"

I give her the breakdown of my crazy night, the hand-touching competition as a finale. "What do I do?"

Like it's the most obvious thing in the world, she says, "You enjoy it! His cousin is equally as hot as Gabriel although in a more rugged way, obviously. But Paige, if they're fighting over you, you know what I say? May the best man win!"

I moan, "You don't understand. I am not in a place where I can deal with this right now."

"Why not?"

Staring at the wall I freeze. "Because, I'm very busy."

Laughing, she says, "You are not! You haven't been on a date in like six months. All you do is work and read, work and read, work and read. I'm sorry, but you need this right now. I have to go. Carter just put his hand down my pants." She hangs up.

Muttering to myself, "Well, that's one way to get her attention, Carter," I turn to the mirror and pause.

Those two guys are really fighting over me for their own egos. I'm nothing special. Just a normal girl with a so-so face and huge fucking problems. I'm not even going to reapply my lipstick. What's the point?

Walking back through the restaurant I turn a corner and see Gabriel leaning over our table, furious.

Ben isn't taking the bait. He's sitting back with a confident, relaxed look. "You're too volatile for her, Gabriel."

I clear my throat to make my approach known.

Their heads turns at the same time, both wondering how much I overheard and neither asking. It takes my breath away how handsome they both are.

Every move Gabriel makes has the grace of a panther and he kind of looks like one, too, with his black hair, black wardrobe and ethereal eyes.

Ben is like a Grizzly bear with his soft brown hair and seemingly harmless resting face, but this morning I saw how he is when poked.

These two in a cage would be a scary thing to behold.

But panthers are quicker, and Gabriel rises out first to take my hand and guide me back to my place in the booth. But before he does he pauses, eyes locked with mine.

"I ordered you one of all the desserts."

"Every single one of them?"

"Didn't know which you liked," he smirks, bringing my fingers to his lips.

Ben groans, "Come on! Laying it on a little thick!"

Gabriel ignores him, but his eyes flicker. I swallow hard and slide onto the leather. Their shot glasses are empty.

"I'll have one more shot." I mutter, overwhelmed.

Ben decides this is his moment — he'll be the one to fetch me that drink. He flies out of the booth, says "I'll be right back," and strolls to tell the waiter what I need. His posture says he's proud of himself for beating his cousin to it.

Gabriel grabs my clutch bag and my hand and yanks me out of the booth, saying under his breath, "Come on!"

My high heels threaten to topple me onto the carpet as I'm half-dragged along. "What are you doing? You're not leaving him here, are you?"

"Fuck yes I am!" Gabriel growls, pushing the back door open and digging his phone from his pocket and dials.

"My heels!"

He looks at my feet, stops and picks me up before I can react. "Hold this to my ear!"

I do as I'm told as he rushes us around the side of the building, me bouncing in his arms. "Mags! You gave them my credit card number? Well, do it. I just took off out the emergency exit, and I need to pay the bill. Do it now! I'm hanging up!" He looks at me. "Hang up for me."

I hear her say, "I swear, this job is never boring," right before I hang up.

He jerks his chin at the driver waiting in a reserved spot by the front door, and whisper-yells, "Start the car!"

Setting me down with all the grace a panther is known for, he whips open the door and ushers me in.

I scoot over in a hurry. "I can't believe we're doing this!"

Gabriel flies into the stretch limo, shouts, "Drive!" and slams the heavy door as we screech away.

GABRIEL

*S*pinning around on the leather bench seat I watch Ben running out of the restaurant, searching for us, and mutter to myself, "Oh, I'm gonna hear about this."

"From who?" Paige asks, those smoky brown eyes of hers fixed on me. The more she drank the more her talons retracted and the real Paige came out. Everything she had to say was interesting, and she didn't just talk for no reason. During our meal she'd listen and add her opinions and ideas, just like she did with that philosophy on why people do drugs. I'm trying to remember why I called her a bitch, but I've got her intoxicating scent in my nostrils and on my clothes from when I carried her, so the reason is buried in the excitement of our escape.

Her lavender dress is hiked up on her left thigh. She sees me looking at her bare knee and reaches to cover up. Delicate fingers push the fabric down and that subtle move is more erotic to me than when that groupie snapped her hot pink garter belt against her hip last Monday night.

"You didn't answer me."

"What did you say?" I'm staring at her lips. This girl pisses me off as much as she turns me on.

"Who are you going to hear about this from?"

My hand hovers near her leg. Her breath hitches. Both of us are watching my fingers, wondering what I'm going to do. I'm waiting for her permission or a sign that she's not going to slap me again. Pulling my hand away I rake my hair back and attempt to relax in my seat despite the erection pushing on my zipper.

"I liked what you said about drugs and spirituality."

"Are you teasing me, Gabriel?"

"No."

"You mean what you're saying?"

"Yeah," I frown, holding her curious look. She makes me nervous. Now that I'm alone with her I don't know what to do if it's not to seduce her. So I decide to try.

As my hand heads her way again she grabs it, gently but still firm, and lays it on my thigh. "Don't. I'm sure you hear the word 'yes' all the time. But I don't look at sex like a lot of people do."

My eyebrows twist my forehead. "I can't wait to hear this."

Paige laughs, "That's a conversation I'll save for another day."

"You think there will be another day?"

"No," she flatly says, then looks out the window as if the subject is closed.

I stare at the side of her beautiful face, every curve delicate. She's not model pretty or trashy hot. She feels like warm milk, especially with that soothing voice of hers. Even when she's nervous, something about her feels grounded and centered. Like she doesn't need my opinion of her to tell her who she is. In fact, she doesn't give a shit what I think about her. Never met a woman like that before. Ever.

"You been teaching yoga long?"

Glancing over to see if I'm really asking or just baiting her, she decides I'm worth a response and says, "Three years, but I've been practicing since I was fifteen."

She pauses to see if I'm bored.

I cock my head to communicate that I want her to continue, go deeper with her answer.

A fresh, shy smile appears and she takes a purposeful breath. "Some very difficult things happened in my family when I was a kid. I needed a way to find peace. Therapy didn't seem cool – I was just a teenager."

"Right," I nod.

"So I went to a yoga class and found that when I was forced to pay attention to my body, everything sort of went away. Things didn't feel insurmountable to me anymore. Holding the Warrior poses gave me a sense of inner strength, which is exactly what they're meant to do. Holding stretches for long periods of time helped me release tension and remember who I am, that peace of mind starts with me." She thinks a moment and sighs, "I'm glad you asked me this because I've forgotten lately. When I was in class as a fifteen-year-old, it was the first time where I wasn't thinking about anything else but my Self, in the literal and spiritual sense of the word. Until then I was always thinking about everyone else and it was exhausting!" Searching my eyes to see if I understand she touches between her breasts. "I was able to get in touch with the still, small voice in here, the one who always knows what to do."

"Did it make your family problems go away?"

A shadow passes over Paige's eyes and she gives a regretful, tiny, shake of her head. "No. But it gave me a way to deal with them. It's all about perception. If you feel like everything is terrible, then it is." Thoughts pass over her eyes as she turns and stares ahead.

"You okay?"

"Mmm."

Yeah, I didn't believe that for a second. But as I go to ask her what's on her mind the glass divider lowers. "Excuse me Mr. Cocker, is there anywhere you want to go?"

"Ha! We're just driving around aimlessly, aren't we? You know what, take us to the old mill in Roswell."

Paige glances to me in surprise. "That's not part of the contest thingy."

"Thingy?" I smile as I dig my phone out. I've got text messages from Ben, Maggie and Elijah. "We've left that contest thingy behind a long time ago, Paige. Hang on, I have to reply to these."

To Ben:

Of course I paid the check. I'm sneaky but I'm not a dick. You're the dick.

To Maggie:

Date's going better than planned. Now leave me alone.

But as I start typing a response to my brother, my thumbs won't move until I put it on airplane mode. Guess this resentment to his not being there tomorrow night isn't dead yet. "First time I've done this in months."

"What?" Paige asks.

"Turned my phone off." I rise off the seat to slide it into my back pocket. Meeting her eyes I hold her confused look. "You think I'm playing you?"

"Yes."

I stare out the window wondering how to convince her. "Alright ask me anything you want." We lock eyes and I give her a lopsided smile that I know the ladies love. "Anything you want, ask. I won't lie."

"When was the last time you slept with someone?"

"Can't remember."

"You said you wouldn't lie!"

Adjusting in the seat I shrug, "Not lying. I never sleep with anyone. They get attached."

She blinks as comprehension drifts in. "Oh. But I didn't mean that. Although that's good information because *wow* on so many levels. I meant sex, Gabriel."

"Then you should have said sex." She waits for my answer and I smirk, holding her eyes. After maybe ten seconds I lean a little closer. "I'm not answering that question."

"You said ask anything!"

"Didn't say I'd answer."

She jumps in her seat. "God!"

"Too easy a joke to say, *Yes*?"

Stifling a laugh she side-eyeballs me. "I'm just going to assume that it was very recently that you *didn't sleep* with someone, and ask you something deeper. Why did you go into music?"

"Because I had to." Pushing my hair behind my ear I confess, "Now this I could talk about all day. If I don't write songs I feel itchy like something's wrong. I have to put words to the page. The melody is in my head before the lyrics sometimes. I have to sleep with a notepad by my bed because just when I'm about to fall asleep a line will come to me, and more often than not it's so perfect I know it came from somewhere other than here." I point to my head.

"It's the getting quiet so you can hear that I was talking about with yoga," she offers.

"Exactly. I related to everything you said about your practice. There's so much noise all day long. And the chatter in here..." I jam the finger into the side of my head. "It's so fuckin' loud like it's trying to keep you from creating, on purpose. Every day I have to fight this noise inside my head, get to the center of the storm so I can write what the Muse tells me to write."

"You believe in that, in the Muse?"

"Oh yeah! You kidding? She is as real as you and me. You can't see her but she's always there. Ever read *The War of Art*?"

She tilts her head. "You mean *Art of War* by Sun Tzu?"

"Nah, Steven Pressfield turned it around. It's a play on words. *The War of Art* is about the Resistance we all have inside us. It was written originally for artists but it applies to everyone. He says in the beginning, I think it was the prologue, that if everyone did what they wanted to do with their lives there would be no need for anti-depression meds, abuse, addiction, overeating, divorce, and the list goes on. People would be following their sense of purpose, their joys not their fears. But the Resistance is powerful. It's the demons we all have that tell us we can't do the thing we want to do." Paige is really listening to what I'm saying, not just waiting for her chance to talk. I jab my head again. "I have to quiet those. They're silent when I'm writing. When I'm onstage. When I'm in the studio recording with Uncle Jason. All their annoying chatter and bold-faced lies quiet down because they can't fight the light. But they don't tell you that. You feel it when you choose it."

She's smiling at me and my gaze drops to her lips. She's got nothing on them, just her natural color, the skin smooth and kissable.

It's all I can do to stay where I am.

"I've read the book, Gabriel."

"Shut up."

"I have!"

Laughing, I lean away from her. "Why'd you have me say all that then?"

"I wanted to hear what you took away from it."

"Prove it. Tell me something I didn't say."

A grin flashes as she glances down. "The amount of Resistance is in direct proportion to the importance of the thing you're meant to do."

"You have read it! What the fuck?"

I laugh, and she joins me.

As we settle down she bites her bottom lip then shrugs, "I can be sneaky, too."

My smile stays where it is as I watch the car head down the sharp decline into the parking lot of the mill. We're the sole car here since the place is closed after dark. The driver slows and rolls the divider down again. "Park anywhere, Mr. Cocker?"

"Farthest in you can go."

Edged with concern, Paige looks out the window. "We're not supposed to be here."

"So what? I practically lived in these hiking trails as a kid. I could show you the way with only a slivered moon in the sky. My mom took us here whenever dad was forced to work weekends and she refused to join him so we wouldn't end up raised by a nanny. My cousins came with us a lot."

"So…is Ben going to show up here, too?"

"Not funny," I mutter as the car slows to a smooth stop. The driver looks at me through the rearview, silently asking if I want to open my own door again. "You learn quick. Yeah, stay there. Oh, hey, what's your name?"

"Larry Monroe."

"I'm Gabriel. This is Paige."

She waves at him, "Hi."

"You have something to keep you busy for a while, Larry?"

"Have an audiobook on my phone. I'm learning how to manage my finances."

Pursing my lips on a nod, I climb out, "Okay then, won't worry about you."

This time Paige slides her fingers onto my offered palm without hesitation. She stands up and is about to let go but I entwine our fingers instead and shut the door.

"You going to slap me again?"

She tightens her hold, making my heart pick up speed.

Above us moths circle the lampposts' yellow light.

The car engine turns off behind us and soon the chirping song of cicadas harmonizes from nearby trees.

"They're so mysterious, aren't they?" She glances up to me. "Oh, you wrote a song called *Cicadas*!"

"On my second album. It's about my Uncle Jaxson and Aunt Rachel, when they were little kids and fell in love."

"I thought it was just a sweet story for the song!"

"Nope, all true. Cool, huh? Here, I'll climb over first." I grab the top railing and throw my legs over the low fence that's really more decoration than boundary.

"This isn't going to be easy with my dress," she mutters, climbing up.

"You're making it look easy."

"No way!" She laughs as she fumbles and sits sidesaddle on it.

"You are the picture of grace."

Rolling her eyes she modestly covers herself. I slide my hands around her waist and lift her up and over, setting her onto the dirt path. She meets my eyes a moment. I have the strongest urge to kiss her.

"It's been so stormy this week," she laughs, starting to walk. "Glad it's clear out."

"Lots of stars," I agree as I look up. Her fingers slide against mine and lock into place. It startles me that she instigated this, so I look over. She flashes a quick smile and my heart starts pounding.

"Do I hear a waterfall, Gabriel?"

"Don't know what you're talking about."

"Oh you don't, huh?"

"Nope." Through the trees to my right comes the unmistakable, crashing cascade of a humongous waterfall. Pulling my phone out with my free hand I turn on the flashlight feature and shine a beam on the water.

Paige gasps, "It's gorgeous!"

"Very."

Glancing to me she tilts her head a little. "Oh, you're so smooth."

"I'm not being smooth. Don't you know how beautiful you are?"

Glancing away she runs self-conscious fingers through her hair as she shakes her head. "Stop it."

"No." I put the roar of the water behind me and tenderly cup her chin. "You going to slap me if I kiss you?"

"I don't know."

"Well I'm going to find out," I rasp, and lean down. Hovering near her mouth I feel the warmth of her skin. I trace my finger up her neck. She searches my eyes like she doesn't know what to do. Our lips brush as I ask, "You ready for this?"

"Are you?"

"No, not at all." I kiss her and feel that same crazy sensation all over again, like this is right where I'm supposed to be.

Her response is tentative at first like she thinks she should hold back. Then her arms float up, fingers gently slipping into my hair. Our jaws unlock as the kiss deepens. Only this time it isn't for the benefit of the reporters. Nobody is here but us and I'm wondering if her pulse is racing like mine is.

Electricity shoots down my chest. I'm getting harder by the second. Hungry for more my hands slowly travel down her sides, exploring her curves. Her breath hitches as I hover near her thighs.

"Okay, that's enough," she breathes, letting me go.

"Fuck," I mutter in awe as I adjust myself. She laughs like she's embarrassed I'm fixing my erection in front of her. "What? I'm not apologizing for this. That kiss...you turn me on."

"Gabriel..." She gives me the sweetest smile.

I pull her to me and kiss her one more time. Her tongue touches mine and suddenly I've got images of tearing this dress off her. I pull away and try to get ahold of myself. Under my breath I rasp, "Never felt like this. I want you so bad it's crazy."

"We just met!"

"Like that ever mattered before," I chuckle, wiping my brow because I've begun to sweat. "I've fucked before I even knew first names."

Paige mumbles, "Well, there will be plenty of girls at the concert tomorrow who will help you with that, and it won't be me. No no no." She smoothes her dress down, not that it needs it. She freezes as she looks up at me. "What?"

"You. Me. Out of here. We've gotta go." Taking her hand I head back for the car at a fast clip.

"Slow down! I'm in heels, remember? This isn't paved!"

"We've gotta get out of here."

"Why?" She tugs hard on my hand.

I whip around, pull her to me and groan as I struggle not to grind, but her hip just hit my erection and it felt way too fucking good. "I want to rip your dress, Paige, and this urge is primal and it's strong and I need you safely back in the car now." I pick her up and throw her over my shoulder.

"Gabriel!"

"Just be quiet. This is for your own good. I want to nail you so bad it's killing me. But you said no. And I'm listening despite how much I want to fuck the shit out of you."

She doesn't make a sound the whole rest of the way.

PAIGE

On the ride back home, Gabriel won't look at me. We're sitting as far apart as two people can. I'm stunned by what he said and by my own restraint, too.

Kissing him felt like nothing I'd ever experienced, but then again I've never been kissed by a rockstar before. There's a history of false intimacy attached since I've loved his music since he first came onto the scene.

You don't really know him.

It just feels like you do.

Don't forget he was a jerk earlier.

Like a mantra I repeat this because my body is buzzing with desire, my hands itching to slide his belt off.

I felt his bulge against my hip back there and now it's all I can think about.

I want to fist his hair.

Tell him to go for it.

Rip my dress off, Gabriel.

Just do it.

Yeah, right.

What a mess that would be.

Tomorrow I'd be at the concert with Shelby and things would be awkward. Like an idiot I'd be waiting for a sign that…God, it's ridiculous to even think about it!

And he'd act all casual then leave town, continuing his tour, next stop Canada of all places, which isn't at all close by.

The fact that I memorized his tour stops before she even called into the radio station is sign enough that I must keep my legs closed.

Shelby was right when she called me out on my playlists — I've got all of his albums. It's just, my life is a fucking disaster, that's why I've been so closed off to him. Plus he was a total jerk! And he called me a bitch to my face! Who does that? Especially in the South?!

I look over and see him gnawing on his cheek, a heavy frown on his face. Glancing to his crotch my eyes widen on the size of his bulge. Feeling me staring at him, he glances over and cocks his eyebrows. "Yeah?"

"Rip my dress off, Gabriel. Just do it."

His eyes sharpen like an animal given the order to attack. He rolls the glass divider down and tells the driver, "Larry, go the long way. Don't stop until I tell you to, even if you pass her apartment."

"Yes, Sir."

Hitting a button the glass divider is covered by a solid black one, giving us total privacy. He tears his blazer off and throws it on the floor.

Suddenly Gabriel is on me, his hands gripping me so tight as he stares at me like he's making sure I meant that. He grabs my dress with both hands, rips it and pulls the sleeves down so that my arms are captured and my boring white bra, exposed. His lips latch onto my neck and I moan as he half-kisses, half-chews his way down, igniting every nerve ending along the way. Before I know what's happening our lips are locked and we're moaning into each other's mouths, grinding pelvises, my legs around him as he kneels in front of me.

"Fuck!" He shakes his head. "You feel too good. I can't take it."

I don't care if he says that to every girl.

Right now he's saying it to me.

I'm the one who frees my breasts from the strict confines of this bra. Gabriel looks down and just when I'm wondering if they're good enough for him, he lunges for the right one, licking it and sucking my nipple until I'm moaning and out of my mind with need. He switches to the left, skillfully massaging as he licks.

He looks up at me and groans, "You're bucking against my erection, Paige. You want something?"

"Yes!"

He rises up and pulls my hair, searching my eyes with the sexiest smile. "What do you want?"

"Don't do this to me. Just…"

"Just what, Paige?"

My pussy is literally throbbing.

But I'm embarrassed. I never dirty-talk.

"Never mind. Forget it."

He bites my bottom lip and locks eyes with me again. "C'mon Paige. Let go. Just say what you want and I'll give it to you."

Aching I close my eyes. "I've never done that before."

"Tell me you want to fuck me, it's okay. Just say it."

I moan, my ass rising off the seat.

He holds my look and grinds a little.

As he backs off I cry out, "Don't tease me!"

"You want my cock, Paige? C'mon baby girl, tell me what you want."

He glides one hand over my panties and murmurs, "You've soaked through these bad boys. Say what you want. I want to give it to you. Drop your inhibition. Let it all go."

Terrified of sounding silly I whisper, "Fuck me. Please fuck me."

Our lips collide. He's kissing me so hard it hurts yet I only want more. I struggle with his belt feeling completely out of my league. His tongue dashes into my mouth as he pulls my panties down my legs and tosses them onto the limo's floor, dipping down to fondle me with his fingers and kiss the damp hair there. Toying with my tender flesh he dips in and runs circles over my swollen clit with his tongue.

I moan and my fingers dig into his shoulders. He dips his tongue inside me and comes out to flick it everywhere inside my lips like he knows exactly what I need, teasing and playing. I start to shake, fisting his hair and rocking against his mouth as a seed of pleasure bursts in me. Everything is pulsing as I whimper, because it's not enough. I want more.

"Gabriel, I need you inside my..."

He looks up with lust in his kaleidoscope eyes. "Say it."

Panting and nervous I murmur, "I need you inside my... pussy."

"Fuck yes," he groans pulling his pants down his thighs and releases a cock that makes my whole body tighten with need.

"You're so big," I moan.

He stares at my mouth, and nods like he's used to hearing that. Taking my hand, he puts it on his length. Groaning he shuts his eyes, rocking his hips back and forth and guiding my fingers, showing me the way. He pulls my ass to the edge of the seat and presses the blunt, mushroom tip up against my pussy, spreading my lips with his fingers. We start kissing as he begins to inch in, but he's so big it's hard for me to relax.

"I'm sorry! I'm trying."

He licks my bottom lip and locks eyes with me, his hooded. He's so handsome I can't believe I'm really doing this with him. His voice is thick and deep, almost gentle. "Let your mind go. It's just you and me here. You feel that? I'm going slow so you can yield to me in your own time. You feel that? You're opening up."

"I feel it," I gasp, spreading my legs more and frowning with pleasure.

"Your pussy is fucking perfect, don't worry. Feel how she's letting me in now?" His eyes roll back in his head as a guttural groan vibrates his chest, eyelids shutting on a deep wince.

I'm stroking his hair and watching his ecstasy. It's such a turn on to think I'm doing this to him.

His mouth reaches for mine and our tongues dance as our hips start moving. With each slow, deep thrust my walls stretch a little more, getting used to his size. He breaks free from the kiss and smiles, panting, "That's good. You're doing great."

As his tongue teases mine I cry out into his mouth. He's hitting something inside that feels so good and overwhelming it scares me. "What's happening?"

He's panting and he looks at me. "That's your g-spot. It feels intense, but let it happen."

"Oh God!" My nails dig into his flesh as I start to tremble. My heartbeat is pounding everywhere. All my baby hairs are standing up. I feel like I might cry. Something is releasing that I didn't even know I was holding onto.

Gabriel kisses my cheek as he keeps a steady rhythm, filling me with each thrust. He murmurs, "I've never felt like this before."

I'm trying to keep from screaming as my pussy bears down on him in hot contractions. He claims my mouth in an amazing kiss, groans and cums with me. Tearing free from my lips he roars, "Holy fuck! What is going on?!"

I am a trembling mess.

Please God, help me let go of him when the time comes.

Or if you're feeling kind, help me keep him.

GABRIEL

*S*hit, I'm in big trouble. I shouldn't have done that. This isn't good. I kiss Paige and look at her, wondering what the fuck I'm going to do now. She's smiling at me like she's in love, looking so goddamn beautiful it hurts. But I'm not ready for this. Anybody in my family would tell her that. And if they meet her, they'll warn her.

Which of course reminds me of Ben.

That fucking asshole tried to swoop in on my date. He spotted how special she is. He's no dummy. But I could kill him right now. Just the idea that he tried has jealous possessiveness charging through my veins.

"Why do you look angry all of a sudden?" Paige asks, pulling up her panties and glancing to her broken dress. "Oh um…"

I scoop my blazer off the floor and hand it to her. "Wear this."

"I need a tissue or something."

Digging through the liquor cabinet I discover a supply of cocktail napkins. "Will these do?"

"Yes, thank you." Shyly she smiles, folding them and tucking them in. "We should have used a condom."

"Ya think?" I mutter before meeting her eyes and seeing the smile disappear from her face. "Sorry, it's just...we should have."

"Yeah, I know," she chuckles, trying to act like she's fine.

But this girl isn't the type you fuck and don't worry about afterward like you do those groupies who go from one singer-songwriter to the next, who even fuck whole bands. Those girls get off on the numbers. They're almost like guys – no real feeling behind it. All they want to do is collect and compare star-level names.

What Paige and I just did wasn't like that at all. It had a shitload of feeling to it. I gave her a part of me, I felt it. Now I don't know what to do with myself. I feel like an open wound.

"I uh...guess I should take you home."

Paige pauses and says, "Guess so."

She's staring at me and I can't look at her. Forcing myself, I offer a smile that doesn't last. She turns to the window and sighs, tugging my blazer tighter around her.

"I can't let my brother see me like this."

Frowning I ask, "Why would he?"

"We live together."

Blinking as I picture her greeting him like this, I groan, "No fuckin' way is that going to happen. Let me think a second." We ride along in silence until I mutter, "I've got it. Hang on. I'm going to call my publicist." Digging out my phone I call Maggie who answers immediately, the sound of the television in the background.

"How'd it go?" she asks, not sounding optimistic.

"I need you. We're coming to your place."

"We?"

"Paige is with me. I need your help."

Alarmed she says, "Come over. Carrie and I are awake."

Hanging up I push the button for the divider. As soon as he can hear me I tell him, "Larry, in three blocks, take a right at Defoor. I'll tell you where to go from there. I don't remember the number, but I can get there by sight." He nods and I reach over to Paige who is pretty confused. "Trust me?"

She nods and takes my hand.

*R*unning up to the Side-Gabled Cottage Maggie owns, I ring the bell and don't have to wait long. Carrie stands behind Mags as she answers the door, both in pajama shorts and small tank tops. "Lookin' good, ladies," I smile.

"Cut the crap. What's up?"

"I need to borrow you and an outfit. You're welcome to join us, Carrie. Be better if you did."

Maggie crosses her arms and glances to the parallel-parked limo. "Why do you need my clothes for fuck's sake?"

"She asked me to tear her dress so I did."

The women exchange glances.

Maggie mutters, "That's hot." Then asks her girlfriend, "Why don't you do that?"

"I'll go to the gym and bulk up so I have that kind of strength." Carrie rolls her eyes. "Give me a break!"

Maggie sighs, "You and your overly gratuitous sex life, Gabriel. Why should I do this?"

"Paige lives with her brother. She doesn't want to broadcast how this date went."

"Deal with your personal shit on your own. The girls you use up and throw away are not in my job description because if they were I would have to quit from disgust and exhaustion long ago!"

Lowering my voice I hold her eyes. "Mags, I like this one. I don't want her embarrassed or ashamed because of what we did. Please help me."

She sharpens with surprise, blinks to her girlfriend and tries to form words.

Carrie takes over. "We'll get changed and be right out with clothes for her. Is she skinny?"

"She teaches yoga."

"That's a yes. Well, shit. Okay, I've got a sundress that fits anyone. It'll have to do."

"Thank you, Carrie. I'll wait in the car to make sure she doesn't feel alone."

This astounds Maggie even more, and her jaw drops open but still she can't form words. Her tongue is normally razor sharp. This is a first.

Their door stays open as they head inside with Carrie whispering a mocking, "See, miracles do happen."

I stroll back to the limo and climb in, taking Paige's hand as soon as I get settled. Relieved she twines her fingers around mine and we squeeze at the same time. She gives me a small smile and my heart reacts immediately.

This is fucking strange. Never had this happen to me.

I glance over and try to figure her out. She meets my eyes. "Thank you."

"I pay her so she has to help. It's not a big deal."

Paige sucks on her lips and stares out the window.

We watch Carrie stand by while Maggie locks up.

"Are they together?"

"Yep."

The girls climb in and take the bench seat opposite ours. "Hi Paige, we talked on the phone. I'm Maggie. This is my girlfriend, Carrie."

"Nice to meet you," Paige says.

Carrie's eyes are dancing and she runs a hand

through her pink hair, biting her bottom lip as Maggie hands over the new dress. Paige looks around like she's unsure if she should change right here.

She whispers like she feels whorish, "This is very awkward for me," and releases my hand.

To give her the facade of privacy, the three of us avert our eyes.

"What's the plan?" Carrie asks.

Mags is so smart she's already figured my strategy out for the most part. As I stare out the window with my elbow on the armrest she explains, "We had a party at my place. You guys came over after you had dinner. My dog tore your dress."

I interrupt, "I was going to say that I spilled red wine on her and ruined it."

"How do you explain the rip?"

"Why would she keep it?"

Paige sighs, "You can look now. The red wine is perfect. I'll use that. Bobby won't like the other one."

I grumble, "It makes it look like I didn't protect her from the dog!"

Maggie throws her hands up, "Fine!"

"Because if a dog attacked her, I would do something about it."

"Gabriel, there is no dog! Calm down."

Mumbling a few cuss words I lean back on the armrest and stare out as the buildings blur up 14th Street. Mags lives on the outskirts of West Midtown near the apartment Hannah used to share with our cousin Emma. We've got fifteen minutes before we get to Inman Park.

Carrie asks, "Did you guys have fun?" trying to make conversation.

Paige and I share a look.

She smiles, "It's...been interesting."

PAIGE

To give the story credibility, Maggie and Carrie are walking up to my apartment with us. Gabriel almost stayed in the car but changed his mind at the last minute. I don't know why. Ben was right when he warned me that his cousin was volatile. Gabriel runs so hot and cold my skin doesn't know if it's burned or frozen.

The girlfriends are laughing like the fake party is still going on. I'm smiling, trying to act the part, but I can't stop checking in on Gabriel. Every time I look back at him he's staring at me with this expression I can't understand. On the elevator he even reached out and caressed my arm, then shoved his hands in his pockets like he hadn't meant to do that. Or like it was an obligation. Which just feels awful.

"This is me on the right," I say, pointing my chin at

it as I dig for my keys. "Can't believe I fit this much stuff into such a tiny bag. Here they are."

Sliding the key in I hold my breath preparing to lie to my brother.

Our modestly decorated living room is dark, as is the kitchen, so the girlfriends quiet with some over-acted, "Shhhhhh," like they're drunk.

They're enjoying this.

Unlike me.

I'm about to tell them that they can go, that he's asleep so there's no need to explain my outfit or the late hour. But then I see that the door to his bedroom is open. My head cocks left as I walk down the hall, leaving them forgotten behind me as my heart begins to pound.

He has to be home. It's Thursday and his favorite television shows are on tonight.

Not only that but he has no money to go out.

I tentatively say, "Bobby?" while pushing the door open wider.

His bed is as empty as the room.

My shoulders slump as I lean against the wall, groaning, "Oh no!"

Gabriel's voice jolts my body into action. "He's not here?"

Turning around I see him in the doorframe to my brother's room. "Oh! You scared me. Uh, I guess he went to his friend's house. They...play games. It runs late sometimes," I explain with a forced smile.

"Video games?"

"Something like that."

Gabriel raises his voice to tell the girlfriends, "Coast is clear. Stop acting like you're wasted." There's a smile in his voice.

I overhear Maggie telling Carrie, "You were good!"

"You think so? I thought the stumble as we walked in felt real."

"It was very convincing. I reached out for you."

"I know! You weren't just pretending?"

"No, I thought you were really falling."

Gabriel and I are staring at each other, listening to them.

Amused he shakes his head.

All I want to do is check my jewelry box to make sure everything is still there.

"So this is where you live?" He walks into the hall like he's going to explore my room next.

I run in front of him. "Don't go in there. It's a mess."

Maggie calls out, "Gabriel, I need to get home."

I think she did that to save me. Gay or straight, no woman wants someone we're attracted to in our bedrooms until we're damn ready.

He glances to a print of Hawaii on the wall. "This yours?"

"Look," I sigh, glancing to the tattered edges of my beach poster. "I know this dinky apartment is laugh-able compared to wherever you must live. So let's not do this and just say goodnight. I'm very tired."

He frowns, sexy hair falling over his kaleidoscope eyes. "You're funny, Paige. You're trying to get rid of me."

"Am I the first girl to do that?" I chuckle, joking.

With total seriousness he says, "Yes," and holds my look before he turns and strolls out of my apartment. Maggie and Carrie follow him, and they send awkward waves my way.

As the door's about to close, Maggie sticks her curly head back in. "You're still coming to the concert?"

God, I forget all about it.

"I don't know," I admit.

She frowns. "Goodnight Paige."

The closing click of the door behind her is the loneliest sound I've ever heard.

I run into my room, intent on screaming and crying my heart out if I find even one gold necklace missing. I nearly break the hinges as I open my beloved jewelry box. Rifling through it my heart is slamming. But everything's here. Even the box with the tiny emeralds Grandma gave me so that I might make earrings out of them one day. Together they're smaller than half an eraser so I don't know if they have any value, but I bet Bobby would know.

And yet...they're here.

In confusion I put the jewelry box back on my old dresser, eyes darting around in confusion until I spot a post-it note on my unmade bed. Grabbing it I read Bobby's messy scrawl.

Hey sis, hope you had fun. I went to Uncle Taylor's to get away for a couple days and see if he can front us the cash before Monday comes. Love you, Bobby

Re-reading it several times I burst into happy tears and crumple the note to my chest. "Oh, thank you! Thank you, God! Thank you!"

PAIGE

Shelby grabs my hand and squeezes hard as Gabriel looks right at me as he sings, concert spotlights dancing over his gorgeous face, black tank top, leather pants, hot as hell boots. The band is totally into it, too, playing behind him with ecstasy on their faces. Gabriel focuses on the audience again as he leaves our side of the mosh pit and walks stage right, leaning into the mic, his deep voice sending shivers into every female here.

I lean over to whisper to Shelby, "Don't get excited for me! He's looking at everyone!"

With a knowing grin she cups her hand over my ear. "Take your head out of your ass."

Security put us here when we arrived. Maggie orchestrated that, introducing me as a friend, and not 'the contest winner,' which I appreciated. After what she did for me last night I wouldn't want her to suddenly go back to treating me like a stranger. She must feel bad for me, knowing that it's not going anywhere between he and I, even though we had sex. As his publicist and friend I bet she sees a lot of casualties in his romantic life.

But when she looked at me with kindness I knew in my heart that they had talked about me, and that he'd instructed her to treat me with respect. He's letting me down gently which I appreciate. Makes it feel less trashy what we did.

But during the show he's locked his beautiful eyes onto me so many times it's becoming difficult not to hope there might be more to it than that. Am I kidding myself? He's got over two million followers on all the major social media outlets. Not combined but on each one! The number of women – and men! – offering themselves up for a night with him is extremely intimidating. Who am I to think I'm special?

God, look at him. The way he owns that stage is pure star. He works the crowd like they're his instruments. And then out of nowhere he hits these high notes you'd think were impossible for a guy with a voice as deep as his.

He's right.

Gabriel was born to be a superstar.

I feel dizzy watching him.

And every time it hits me that he's leaving for Canada soon, my heart shrivels.

Shelby shouts, "Oh, I was hoping they'd be here!" as

five female hip-hop dancers bounce onto the stage with practiced, sexually explicit moves. I recognize them from his videos, too. One leaves the others and goes right up to him. She's gyrating around him as he stares into her eyes, singing like the song is now for her.

Shelby and I exchange a look as they grind. "You did this to me."

She winces and squeezes my hand. "It's part of the show, that's all!"

The girl gives him the sauciest look and bounces back to rejoin her crew as they form a line behind him to enact fantastic moves that make your heart pound.

They *are* the music.

He *makes* the music.

How can I compete with that kind of connection?

Suddenly I'm very aware of the sexy dress I chose to wear. Why did I even try to be someone else? This isn't me! I'm overselling. Shelby encouraged it when she showed up at my place to get ready. I told her about what happened and she insisted I needed to play up my best attribute – my ass – so that he would leave town thinking about me. But look at those dancers! Their butts are phenomenal, and they've got much bigger breasts than I have.

Shelby looks at me. "Are you comparing bodies?"

"No!"

"Yes you are, I can see it in your eyes. I've been there, don't lie to me!"

"I can't help it. Look at them!"

She and I stare at the girls as they grind on each other. She winces and cups her hand over my ear to say, "They're probably stupid."

It's so funny and ridiculous that I start cracking up. She does, too.

This is why I need her. Bumping her hip I mimic what those dancers do. We do terrible renditions of their dance but have the most fun trying. Glancing to the stage my smile freezes as Gabriel and I lock eyes. He was watching us. He gives me a wink and turns to hold his right arm up as Existence comes to an end.

The dancers hit poses and the band crashes an amazing finale out. The audience goes nuts, but I'm more excited than they are.

That wink was for me.

It wasn't in my imagination.

Shelby grins at me. "I saw!"

"He winked at me!"

"I know," she laughs. "He really did."

PAIGE

*R*ight after the encore Shelbs shouts, "Let's go backstage before we get trampled. Don't fight the river! Go with it!"

We are carried out by the swarm toward the exits and the huge lines at merchandise tables. People are shouting about how good he was. I hear a girl with short hair and a nose piercing say, "You see that dancer who was up on him? That's Olivia. They were photographed coming out of a hotel in Barcelona together last month!"

I snap at her, "Why don't you shut the hell up!!"

She exchanges a look with her friend.

Shelby guides me toward a bouncer. "Okay, let's get you out of here."

"I can't believe I just did that!"

"Me neither." We hold up our wristbands to a huge

dude with tattoos and a walkie-talkie on his waist. Shelby informs him, "We have backstage passes."

He nods and pulls the rope back.

Backstage is a zoo. Gaffers and lighting technicians running around tearing everything down. Dancers laughing as they pass us, talking about what they did right, and who fucked up which cue. The band's roadies are stacking gear while the band rests in a room filled with V.I.P.s. There's booze overflowing, a feast lined against one wall, and Gabriel is nowhere to be seen.

Shelby and I hover for a moment. At the same time we recognize Gabriel's sister Hannah. She's with her husband who we also know from news, a champion MMA fighter. They're sharing a chic lounge chair, talking like there's nobody else in the room.

A deep voice behind me says, "Paige."

I spin around to find Ben smiling at me. He looks incredibly handsome in faded blue jeans and a white Henley shirt, with boots that look like they've been worn every day for twenty years.

Shelby's head cranes up and she nearly faints again, clearly attracted to him. "I'm Paige's best friend, we didn't officially meet."

"Ben Cocker."

She bites her bottom lip and nods, "Shelby," twisting the ends of her tight blonde curls. Carter who?

Blushing I tell him, "Sorry about last night."

His laugh brightens his whole face. "It wasn't your fault." To Shelby he asks, "So you both teach yoga?"

She nearly falls over herself. "Paige teaches more Yin Stretch and Hatha, but I do Vinyasa and sometimes Bikram. Have you ever done…hot yoga?"

He smirks, "I've done every kind there is."

Remembering what he told me I explain, "His family has a retreat on their property, so they've had all kinds of teachers come through there over the years."

"My mom and dad's ranch. They live just a couple miles from my farm." Glancing to me he shoves his hands in his pockets and asks the hard question. "You have fun last night?"

My face flushes deeper red. "Yeah, we just went to the waterfall."

He frowns, "Which one?"

"By the old mill in Roswell?"

"That's a dam, not a waterfall."

I stare at him. "Gabriel didn't say that."

"Probably trying to impress you."

Maggie and Carrie walk up, the former pointing to my best friend and announcing, "Another natural-curls girl! Yes! How often do you wash it?"

Shelby laughs, "No more than every other day, you?"

Maggie grins, "If I wash mine every day, total 'fro.'"

"Can't even deal with the frizz!" Shelby rolls her eyes, looking adorable.

In a declaration or ownership Carrie takes Maggie's

hand. Shelby glances down and subtly reacts, taking a half step back to let it be known she's not trying to hit on anybody, she's just being friendly. Trouble is that Shelby has a hot little yoga body and personality to spare. And like me, she's wearing a mini dress barely covering her.

I can tell Maggie is happy her girlfriend got jealous as she asks me, "Have you seen Gabriel yet?" To Ben she gives him a respectful but disinterested wave. "Hey Ben."

"Hey Mags."

Shrugging one shoulder I tell her, "No, not yet. But he was great out there tonight!"

"Wasn't he? I caught him looking at you a lot, Paige."

"Yeah?" I smile.

"Come on. He has his own dressing room. We'll have some drinks in there." She leads the way with Carrie at her side.

Hannah calls out, "Where are you headed, Ben?"

He raises his voice over the conversations. "His dressing room. You coming? Where's Ethan?"

"He rushed home right before the encore. Can't be away from Charlie too long since she's due any day. We'll join you guys in a minute," she smiles before turning back to Tobias and lowering her volume to a more intimate one.

Shelby and I exchange a look because both of us are thinking the same thing – that the Cockers are one good-looking family. And I am so envious of how

Tobias was gazing at Hannah. They were so connected. I want that.

As we go to leave a group of people pour into the room. Shelby scoots by them but I get pushed backward. Ben touches the small of my back to catch me and keeps his hand there until we're free to go. I glance up. He's locked on me with a confident glint in his eyes. He's definitely interested in me. Gabriel tricking him didn't stop that.

Shelby slows for me to catch up, and she casts a knowing look to Ben, saying under her breath, "You're so lucky."

Maggie is talking outside Gabriel's dressing room to some guy in a suit. "Glad you're happy. Oh, Devin, this is Paige, she won the contest."

He shakes my hand. "Oh yes, saw the photos of you two at Rays on the River. Did you have a nice time?"

"Yes, thank you."

He nods and excuses himself.

Maggie waits until he's out of earshot to tell our group, "Devin is the representative of the record label. He's just here to get laid. That's what everyone wants. Money and tail. It's all they care about." She winks and opens the door.

Out runs Olivia, pulling her shirt over braless, naked tits. "Excuse me!"

Maggie tries to shut the door but inside Gabriel is zipping up his pants. He turns and his gorgeous eyes narrow as he realizes what's going on. He locks on me and his lips slacken.

I take a step back and run into Ben.

Shelby grabs my arm, whispering, "Oh fuck."

Maggie slams the door. "I'm so sorry, Paige, I should've…"

I start running.

Shelby's heels are right behind mine.

Gabriel shouts my name.

He doesn't chase me.

But Ben does.

*M*aggie pushes at me, "Go after her," as passing crew members, roadies and groupies amble by, curiously watching the drama unfold.

I start to do as she says, but then pause, running a hand through my hair as I watch Ben running after her.

Growling I head back into my dressing room.

"What are you doing?" Mags demands as Carrie shuts the door behind us. "Are you sabotaging this on purpose, Gabriel? God, the look on that poor girl's face. You're going to let Ben make her feel better? I saw how he was looking at her. It's not friendship he's after."

Grabbing a beer off the coffee table I smash it against a wall and shout, "He's better for her than I am!"

The girls are quieted until Maggie says, "Gabriel, if you care this much about her…"

"You don't understand!" I shout, rubbing a heavy hand down my face. "We're leaving for Canada tomorrow. Three cities there! Then London, Ireland, Paris! You think I can carry on a long-distance relationship when I've never even had a steady girlfriend in my whole fucking life?" Pointing in the direction they went I bark, "He's stable. Ben's here. He's got a nice quiet farm that's perfect for someone like her. Someone who's grounded. Kind. Smart. Beautiful." Grabbing my head I groan through my fingers, "Jeezus, he does fucking yoga like she does! They're perfect for each other!" I collapse on the couch and meet Maggie's impatient eyes. "And I'm just…me."

Carrie shuffles her feet and glances to her girlfriend as Mags crosses her arms. "So what are you going to do tonight?"

"Go home and sleep."

Snorting she shakes her head. "That's not what I thought you'd say."

"What, you expect me to invite a bunch of dancers to my loft?"

"After what you just did, yep!"

I glare at her. "Go home, Mags."

She marches to the door and holds it open for Carrie, slamming it behind them.

My torso is in knots, eyes dead. Can't even see the room. Don't remember the show except for Paige's face staring up at me like it was just us out there. She doesn't know me like my brother and sister do – I'm not the type of guy you can hang a fragile heart on. I've never called anyone my girl.

The door opens and I glance over to see Olivia is back. "Word backstage is I caused some mad-drama."

I clasp my hands behind my head. "This place is worse than my family's grapevine."

Clicking the door shut she enters with an apologetic look. "Hey, I'm sorry, I just did our normal routine after a show. I didn't know you had a girl out there tonight."

"It just happened. You couldn't have known."

"Is it serious?" she asks, stunned. "When I took off my shirt and unzipped your pants, you whacked my hands away." Under her breath she says, "And me half-naked like a dumbass. I mean, at first I thought it was because you thought I danced badly out there or something."

Dropping my hands I throw a boot on the table and mutter, "Nah, you always dance great."

"You like this girl?"

"Doesn't matter."

Olivia stares at the floor a second, then motions between us as she raises her eyes. "So nothing's going to come of this, is it?"

"I thought you knew that."

Biting her lip she shakes her head. "Now I do." She goes to leave.

I jump off the couch, walking fast. "Olivia, hang on."

"It's okay, Gabriel. Forget it."

Planting myself between her and the door I bend my knees to engage her attention, forcing her to look at me. "Don't do that. I know you're tough, but don't act like that." She stares at me. "Don't quit on me. The show needs you. You and the girls are family now, right? We've got a long run ahead of us. I need you. Don't look away. I mean it. I need you here."

She swallows and nods. "I don't *want* to leave everybody."

"Then don't." I pull her to me and kiss the top of her head. She pats my back as the door opens and slams into me.

Hannah says, "Oh, sorry!"

Olivia hurries out. Tobias and Hannah watch her and as soon as we're alone, Tobias says, "Let me guess. Unrequited love."

"Just something that had to end."

Hannah laughs as she heads to grab beers for them out of my fridge. "The day you fall in love will be the day Dad hates politics."

I mutter an irritated, "So never, Hann? That's harsh shit right there."

"When you have women throwing their panties at you, who literally will fuck you anywhere you demand it, how can you settle down with one? I mean, maybe when you're in your fifties and all of this doesn't matter to you anymore."

I stare at her, numb. "I'll never retire from music."

"And you'll probably never retire from being a player."

"Tobias gave up women to be with you. He has almost as many fans as I do."

She laughs, "Half as many."

Her husband takes a beer from her and pops the top, handing it back before taking one for himself. "He's right. I could easily fuck anyone I want."

"Tobias!" she cries out, eyes wide.

He shrugs, "But I choose not to, because I've got someone who's worth being faithful to." Locking eyes with me he says with a frank tone, "Never gonna be anybody I could love more than your sister. It's just not possible, so why fuck this up?"

She melts and slides her arms around him, kissing him like I'm not here. "I adore you."

"I know," he smirks, slapping her ass.

They're always like this.

I normally don't care.

This time it's painful.

Shutting my eyes I lean against a wall and curse Ben.

"Where is everybody, Gabriel?"

"What?"

"I asked where the family is. Where'd you go?"

"A lot on my mind," I mutter. "Uh...Elijah's dining with God. I told Mom not to come. It weirds her out seeing panties thrown at my head. Dad took her out to dinner to make her feel better for missing it. Max and Caden were here. They said hey then split because they had dates with them and didn't want the girls ogling me. Eric's with the Falcons for Spring Training I guess. Lexi..."

When I don't finish the sentence Hannah says, "Lexi what? And where's Emma, Zoe, Nicholas, Wyatt, Hunter, Nate? Sofia isn't here and she's just one town over."

"What's your fucking point?"

"They should all be here. You're in Atlanta for one night."

"I offered them tickets. Everyone's got their own lives."

"I'm sorry, but the cousins who are in high school would normally die to be at something like this. But..."

"But what?!"

"You're an island unto yourself, that's what!"

Walking to the door I correct her, "You know what, Hann, it was just me and Elijah before he went to Yale." I grab the knob with my beer bottle barely hanging on as I search for my keys. "When you're a twin, you arrive in life with a best friend already attached. You, Ben, Ethan, Sofia Sol, Emma, and even Eric most days, all you guys stuck together growing up. Elijah and I weren't in that group. Same with Max, Caden, Nicholas and their siblings under them. They stuck together. So it was me and my brother and that's it. Get off my fuckin' case because if anybody is aware that someone's missing from this room, and *that there's a hole in my life,* it's me. Because my twin should be here right now. And I don't need you kicking my dick in the dirt over how the cousins feel about me. You're making me feel like a piece of shit. Good night."

Long strides take me out of my dressing room. Along the way friends try talking to me. Shaking my head I mutter, "Tomorrow, guys. Hit me up then."

Hannah shouts, "Gabriel!"

"No!" I throw my arm up without looking back or slowing these angry footsteps down.

PAIGE

*S*helby's scrolling through her phone. "I'm looking up that Olivia chick."

"What's the point, Shelbs. Just leave it alone."

Ben motions to the parking lot where fans still congregate hoping for a glimpse of their hero. "Let's grab a drink somewhere. You guys don't want to go home feeling angry like this. The bar at JCT kitchen has a patio where we can cool down."

Swallowing hard I glance to Shelby who is obsessed with what she's reading. "There are tons of photos of them." She goes to show me but I push the phone away.

"No way. I can't look."

The three of us walk under lamps with moths floating in their light, reminding me of the parking lot by the mill. And just to kick me when I'm down, cicadas break into song, harmonizing with each other.

Ben guides us to a Jeep. "This is me." Off my confusion he explains, "The truck is my second vehicle. I was bringing crates in from the farm when I…hit your car." A sexy lopsided smile appears. "Rammed into you? Is that better?"

"It's closer to the truth," I smile.

He holds his hand out to help Shelby get in first. Then me. "You okay?"

Not one bit, but I'm not a whiner.

"I'm fine. Just tired."

He gazes at me like he doesn't believe my lie. I take his hand and let him help me up.

As he walks around to get in, Shelby whispers from the backseat, "Ben is super dreamy, Paige."

Her eyes go dead as I look at her like she really needs to shut up now. As he climbs in she asks, "You have a farm?"

Thick fingers turn the key in the ignition. "Organic vegetables and fruits. My dad always wanted to grow them, but he ended up doing dairy and cage free eggs instead. We only have so much time, you know?" He glances to me as he pulls out of the lot, then fixes a steady gaze on the road as he mutters, "Life doesn't always follow your plan."

Shelby keeps him engaged in an easygoing conversation as we drive to the restaurant. I'm glad he chose it even though I'm not a fan of the main dining room. It's high-end and stuffy there. But the upstairs bar and patio are the opposite. The younger crowd gravitates to them for the playlist, cheaper menu, and fire-pits.

On a warm night like this they'll be blazing just for cool-factor alone. Everyone loves fire.

I stare out at the Atlanta skyline but all I see are bare breasts bouncing out of his dressing room, and the way he slowly zipped his pants like he wasn't in a hurry.

There was shock when he saw me.

Did he forget I was there?

A tear slides down my cheek and I brush it away, unseen.

We pull into the parking lot and I overhear Shelby asking, "Did you call your insurance company already?"

Ben's arm is draped over the steering wheel as he scans the lot for an empty space. "Called as soon as I left your work."

That's one more thing to make me feel like a failure. "I forgot to call!"

"You still have time," he reassures me. "And I told them it was my fault." He expertly parks the car so smoothly Shelby and I might as well be standing on solid ground. "Wait there."

As he walks around the Jeep Shelby whispers, "Paige, he's better than dreamy."

"I know he is, but..."

The door opens and Ben offers me his hand. "You didn't have to bring us here to make me feel better."

As my heels stabilize on the asphalt he smiles into my eyes. "Yes I did."

He offers his hand to Shelby and helps her down next, shutting the door and walking between us. She keeps him busy with more easy conversation, a skill she's always had.

I'm glad Carter isn't here. Her boyfriend is hipster-cute. His thighs are the size of Ben's biceps. He'd be threatened seeing how Shelby gazes at Gabriel's cousin, and I honestly don't think she can help it. She keeps urging me to date Ben but it's obvious she's very into him.

Digging my phone out I check for messages from Gabriel or Maggie, but nobody has reached out. Guess it's over just like that. One surreal roller coaster of a night then poof...I'm forgotten.

Shelby glances to me and raises an eyebrow, silently asking. I shake my head and hide the phone before I become obsessed. "I haven't been here in a while."

Ben agrees, "Last time I was here my cousin Ethan and I sat on the patio and we watched a hurricane."

"You did?" I ask, eyes widening. "That must have been amazing!"

Laughing under his breath, "Yeah, he and I enjoy that stuff. But what came afterward was a bigger storm than that."

Shelby asks, "Sounds exciting! Tell us!"

Biting his lip he thinks about whether or not to go there. He's walking between Shelby and I, the parking lot quiet because everyone's already here at this hour.

Atlanta is not a late city. Only a pair of headlights shines in the distance and they're leaving.

He sees we're interested and says, "Alright I'll tell you."

Shelby and I listen and react to every twist and turn of the crazy story. As he guides us to the small couches being vacated by a group of guys in khaki shorts and polo shirts, he asks, "You didn't hear about it? It was all over the news. I hated every second of that media coverage. Had to disappear into my farm to remember who I was when it was all over."

"We never watch the news," I tell him over loud conversations and a retro 80's playlist.

Shelby explains, "It's all negative and hyped to increase viewership. Not good for the soul."

Ben laughs, "Can't blame you," and asks, "What are you ladies having?"

Thinking about it, I decide to go light. "After the tequila, I'd just like some lemonade. No, wait. Make it a vodka lemonade."

Shelby laughs, "I was going to say!" She smiles up at Ben from her seat. "Vodka cran for me. Oh, let me give you my card."

He walks off, "Yeah right. Put your purse away."

But she's already fumbling through it. "If Carter hears that guy bought me a drink he'll lose it."

"How will he know?"

"*I'll* know and that's enough," she says on a quiet snort as she locks eyes with me. "He is so hot, Paige, I swear to God if you don't take him I will." Her head bobs to her wallet. She rummages around and blinks at it, neck lengthening. "My debit card isn't here," she mutters, digging around some more.

"Did you leave it in your hoodie after class? I do that sometimes."

Shaking her head she digs through all the compartments, even the ones she's checked. "No. I always keep it here because my aunt Joanie told me that how you treat your money is how your money treats you." Meeting my eyes, Shelby says, "I never forgot that. It's always in my wallet."

Staring at her I remember Bobby running from my bedroom with Shelby's purse in his hands last night. My throat goes dry and I rise up on wobbly knees. "I have to go to the bathroom. Will you excuse me?"

"Don't be so formal, Paige. It's just me."

Just you who doesn't know about my brother's gambling problem and that he didn't come home last night after you told him to grab your purse for you.

"Sorry," I mutter, snatching my small clutch bag up with shaky fingers. "I'm nervous from Ben, Gabriel, everything." Rushing off I search my contacts and hit the call button.

Uncle Taylor answers, "Paige! Well now, kiddo! What a surprise. And on a Friday night? Aren't you supposed to be partying like all the girls your age?"

I croak, "Is Bobby with you?"

He pauses. "No, I haven't seen your brother since Christmas. Why?"

Everything spins as I whisper, "He said he was visiting you. He's not there?"

With concern he hesitates and slowly says, "Bobby's not here. Is he in trouble? Are you okay?"

Lying has never come easy to me and now is no exception. "He's probably gone away with some girl. We were supposed to watch a movie, that's all."

"Oh, well, can't blame him for not wanting to check in with you. A boy's gotta become a man someday, you know? Come and go as he pleases. Can't have his older sister looking out for him the rest of his life!"

"Yeah, I'm sure that's it," I whisper. "Sorry to bother you, Uncle Taylor." I hang up while he's talking and stare at the cement below my feet. Is it supposed to be moving like that?

Ben is sitting next to Shelby when I hobble back. She's smiling at him like she's forgotten all about her missing debit card.

"Shelby?"

She glances to me and her smile fades. "Paige, you're pale. You okay?"

"Bobby stole your debit card last night."

She blinks at me, then a frown slashes her forehead. "What?! Why?" She and Ben stand up as she swims in confusion. "Are you sure? I mean, why would he do something like that?"

Over the sharp lump in my throat I drop the bomb

I've been hiding for so long. "He has a gambling problem."

"You didn't think to warn me when I said, *Bobby get my purse?* Are you crazy!?"

"He doesn't normally steal. I mean, he hasn't for a couple years. I was so nervous about the date I wasn't even thinking!"

She stares at me. "Oh well that's good to know! He doesn't normally but he chose me to fall off the wagon with?"

Ben's voice is low as he takes our arms and guides us away from the patio where people have begun to stare. "Is there a reason why he would do this?"

Numbly I'm staring at Ben when I realize he's leading me to answer the truth that he overheard when we were waiting for Officer Timothy.

Licking my dry lips I tell Shelby, "We're getting an eviction notice Monday." Her eyes are flitting back and forth on mine. "He's trying to win the money to pay for us to stay in our apartment."

Softening she moans in frustration, "Why didn't you tell me that? How come I'm just now finding out about all of this?"

"He's my brother, Shelby."

Ben takes a sharp breath. "She's protecting her family."

"I'm her family, too!" Shelby says, hitting her chest. She looks at me with hurt in her eyes. "I spend more time with you than anyone. I love you like my sister.

Why didn't you tell me you were going to be fucking homeless so I could help you?"

"I was embarrassed. I'm ashamed."

Covering her face, Shelby starts to cry. "I don't know how to feel right now. Betrayed? Left out? Robbed?" Her hands drop as she asks in a pleading voice, "Is it possible he'll win?"

"Maybe?" As she stares at me for the truth, I shake my head. "He never leaves when he's winning."

"Paige, I have to call the police!"

Ben pulls out his phone.

She asks him, "Are you calling the cops?"

Tears fly up as my heart leaps into my throat.

PAIGE

Shelby and I barely spoke all day at work. Her consistently bubbly nature was absent, and people noticed.

As she counts the register and I turn the sign around in the window after closing, she asks, "Have you heard from him yet?"

"Bobby?"

"No, Ben. Did he call or text you? Did his uncle find your brother? I would think you'd have told me if he called but since you don't tell me important things I didn't want to assume."

Rolling my eyes I mutter, "He texted the search was still on."

Shelby exhales through her nose and keeps counting.

I walk from room to room and turn the lights out.

She doesn't even have the music playing. It's as if

we're working in a morgue. "Did you sleep last night, Shelbs?"

"No. You?"

"Not at all."

She glances up from the money. "You look sick."

"I haven't eaten."

Her eyebrows twitch as she goes back to counting, as if to say I deserve this.

"I should have told you."

"Ya think?" she saltily mutters. "I can't believe you kept all this from me."

"It's not like you and Carter have room for us. And up until last week I thought we had enough money to get by and beg the landlord for another month of patience. But then Bobby gambled the money he'd just earned on a small house painting job, so what was I going to do?"

She shoves the register closed. "You know, you've always said I'm family to you but you don't treat me like that when it comes to your blood family."

"Shelby…"

"NO! It's true, and it makes me feel like shit. If you have problems I want to know about them. That's what best friends are for."

Walking to my purse I mumble, "Then it would have been both of us feeling awful. It's not like you had the money to loan me."

"Well I ended up giving you guys all the money I had anyway, now didn't I!" She grabs her purse as she passes me for the door like she can't get away fast enough. Whipping around she jams a finger in my face. "He took my debit card! He violated me, Paige. We were up on that roof laughing and acting like friends and the whole time he had everything I earned in his pocket! It's so shitty I can't even wrap my head around it."

"I know, it's a disease."

"Fuck that!" she snaps, bursting out the door.

I follow her, "Shelby, don't give up on me!"

Throwing her arms up she shakes her head. "I haven't called my bank to tell them it's gone yet, because I love you that much. I'm giving you and Ben this chance to find that fucking thief and then I really don't know what's going to happen with you and me. I'm just…I'm really hurt. I'm dying here." She walks to her car and climbs in as I watch, helpless.

Locking up the studio I stare inside and see the ghost of our dance party that happened less than a week ago. And now look where we are.

My phone rings as I climb into my dented old car. I jump to answer and see Ben's name on the screen. "Did he find my brother?"

"My uncle finally heard back from his friend in the police department. There are three illegal games happening now, but one has been going nonstop for over a week."

"That's probably the one he was at before. It's gotta be how he knew where to go."

"We're going to check it out tonight when my uncle can get away. My Aunt Jaimie has a charity dinner at The Atlanta Women's Foundation and he's going to head out as soon as she leaves."

"He doesn't want her to worry," I whisper, staring out my windshield. "Why is he doing this for me?"

"Because I asked him to."

"Ben," I groan, laying my head on the steering wheel. "Thank you."

"I'll call you after, tell you if we got him or not."

"I have to be there! I'm going with you!"

"Paige, that's not a good idea. These illegal games are dangerous."

"That's why I have to be there, Ben! If anything happens to Bobby…Don't leave me out of this."

After a moment of silence he exhales. "Fine. I'll text you when I'm on the way to pick you up. I don't know exactly when but it will be sometime after eight."

"You promise?"

"I promise."

Thanking him and hanging up I call Shelby. She waits until the last ring to answer which means she didn't want to. "Yeah?"

"They might have found him. We're going tonight to see, and I didn't want to leave you out."

"I'm coming with!"

PAIGE

Our headlights illuminate the exterior of a dirty warehouse with a row of fancy cars parked out front. There is nobody within a mile of this paint-chipped place. They do not belong here.

"This is where your uncle said it was?" Shelby nervously asks.

Another car pulls up and Ben says "That's him," as he engages the emergency brake and withdraws the key from the ignition.

Exactly as handsome and intimidating as he appears in photographs, Justin Cocker, Gabriel's father and former Senator of Georgia, steps out of a black Audi and straightens his suit jacket as he meets Ben's eyes through the windshield.

We all climb out.

Ben hugs him. "Uncle Justin."

"Glad you didn't try to be a hero and run in without

me." Their voices stay low as they separate. "Did you see my son's concert last night?"

"I did."

"How'd he do? His mom was tearing her hair out with jealousy not being there herself to see it."

Ben's eyes flit to me and he clears his throat. "I thought Aunt Jaimie hates how the girls go all Beatles-nutso over him."

"She does. But she also hates missing it. It's a battle. Being a rockstar's mother isn't easy. That's what she always says. I tell her, *wait until you have a President for a son.*"

Ben chuckles and runs a self-conscious hand through his hair. Now that the polite, Southern chitchat is over, Gabriel's dad stares at the warehouse and I study his face without meaning to. He's a blonde, clean-shaven, older version of his son. They both have the strong jaws, cute nose, intense pale green eyes. And they both feel unreachable.

Sensing I'm staring at him, he glances to me and Shelby for the first time. "Who is the sister?"

I raise my hand halfway. "Me."

"You two are dating?" he asks Ben.

We simultaneously answer, "No."

Shelby helps us out by lying, "I'm dating Ben. It's really new. And she's my best friend. Her brother stole my debit card."

"How'd he know the password?"

"It's my boyfriend's name plus the number one, so… it wasn't hard."

Mr. Cocker cocks a blonde eyebrow. "You have a boyfriend and you're dating my nephew?"

Clearing his throat Ben explains, lying, too, "They just broke up. I kind of fucked things up for them."

Rolling his eyes, Mr. Cocker mutters, "You're just like your father. Let's do this. Ladies, stay here."

Ben's staring after him for a beat like, *what did you mean I'm like my father?* But bigger things are happening so he doesn't push for an explanation as they walk to the door and disappear inside.

After a few minutes, I look at her.

"Shelby, I can't wait out here."

"Yeah, fuck this. What year is it?"

My hands are shaking as I open the door. She and I exchange a look and head in. The air is filled with smoke and we can hear low male voices engaged in tense conversation. I recognize my brother's and suddenly my feet have a mind of their own.

Around the corner we come upon a long oval table with eight players. On one side is the dealer. My brother is on the end with piles of chips in front of him. I don't know their value but he's not losing. He doesn't have the biggest pot. A few other players are ahead, too.

There are three bouncers along the walls waiting to strike now that there's been an interruption from someone who's considered a 'good guy' and doesn't do illegal things like this. They know he has power in high places and they could be in trouble, which they don't want. Things could get very nasty in here. Everyone is watching Mr. Cocker wondering how he found them, and what he's going to do now that he has.

The former Senator is coolly explaining that Bobby is leaving now and to cash out those chips. "I assume we won't have an argument?" he pointedly asks the man who appears to be in charge. This guy looks like he walked off a plantation, his linen suit pale yellow, and a cane rests on his chair. He's Southern old money, most of it dirty if I had to guess.

"I'm not ready to go!" my brother snaps.

Frightened I can't keep quiet anymore. "Bobby...?"

The room goes silent.

All heads turn toward me.

"Paige!" His eyes flit to Shelby and he sinks in his chair.

She is too scared to yell at him, react or even move.

Ben's fists are at his side ready for use.

Mr. Cocker says it again. "Are we going to have a problem?"

"That all depends now, doesn't it, Senator," Yellow Suit says in a thick drawl. "What we're doing is merely for sport, you understand."

Mr. Cocker wears the expression of a man who's seen the dark underbelly of too many illegal situations. "How 'bout this, Franklin? You keep playing and I won't shut down your private 'sport' as long as you promise never to allow Bobby Miller in the game ever again."

My brother jumps out of his chair.

The bouncer grabs him.

I scream his name.

Ben grabs me and holds me in place.

"Shhhh," he whispers.

My eyes are locked on my brother in the arms of that beast, as Shelby starts to cry.

Mr. Cocker eyeballs everyone and settles his calm and steady gaze on the old man as if none of this fazes him. "Do we have a deal?"

Franklin smiles. "I don't enjoy drama at my parties. Remove him." The bouncer wrestles my brother out, breaking my heart every step of the way. "Oh, and Robert?" the old man calls after Bobby, using his whole name in a sleazy way, like he knows him better than I do. The bouncer grabs Bobby's face and makes him listen. "Don't come back…understand? You do and Boone here won't be so gentle. Take him away."

I yank at Ben but he's too strong. "Just wait. He won't hurt him today."

Franklin overhears this. "That's right. Your brother is a lucky boy…today." He nods to someone I hadn't seen before, a man standing against the wall, hands clasped low, one foot casually perched. "Cash him out."

Nobody else at the table has said a word, which is eerie and unsettling. They look like wax figures to me.

Gabriel's father walks to collect the money for my

brother. His trim body is tense as the chips are counted and the cash is placed in his open palm.

"Carry on," he tells Franklin with a single nod.

Shelby hurries out with us as the dealer shuffles. Coming to life, the remaining players pick up their cards as they're dealt. A shiver drifts down my body.

Outside, the bouncer gives a surly scan before he vanishes inside the warehouse.

Bobby doesn't look like himself. He's shifty-eyed like he needs his fix. He's not sure how to behave now that he's been forced to stop when the money hasn't run out.

I've seen this look in our mother's eyes before she joined the rooms of Gambler's Anonymous. I hoped I'd never see it again.

Shaken, Shelby asks, "How much did you take from me?"

His desperation fixates on the cracked asphalt and he won't meet her eyes.

Mr. Cocker asks how much she had in her account. She tells him and he counts from the stack. There's disgust in his eyes as he sneers, "I'm going to assume he cleaned you out. I've known addicts before."

Suddenly angry I take a step forward. "Don't talk about my brother like he's not human! Like he has no feelings! He's right here." Yanking the money from Mr. Cocker's hands I count it out and give Shelby what was stolen. "I'm so sorry."

Silently she takes it.

I quickly count the rest and there's not enough to cover Bobby's share of rent for this month. Mr. Cocker is watching me. I meet his eyes to insist, "It's a disease. He can get help!" as I put my arm around Bobby to ask him, "You okay?"

"No."

"Let's go home."

My voice is uncommonly steady as I tell Mr. Cocker, "Thank you for what you did tonight. I know you didn't have to." I start to leave and realize I don't have my car. But my voice does not falter and my spine stays proud as I ask Ben, "Would you please drop us off? If you don't feel comfortable doing that I can call a Lyft."

"Of course I'll drive you." He guides a stricken Shelby to the Jeep. "Uncle Justin, I'll call you tomorrow."

"Don't tell Rachel what you did tonight. Your father can handle it."

"Mom will never know. Thank you."

Bobby's body has deflated, his urge to fly back inside that warehouse, gone. He gets in the Jeep without a fight and I climb in the backseat with him. Shelby and Ben sit up front. Nobody talks until we get dropped off first.

Ben says, "Bobby?" My brother glances to him. "You ready to be a man yet? Getting help is up to you."

They hold the look before the Jeep pulls away and

harmonious chirping begins to echo off the Dogwood trees.

"The cicadas think they're alone," my brother chokes, on the verge of tears.

Hugging him I whisper, "You're not alone."

GABRIEL

*M*opping the sweat from my face after Montreal's concert I head to my dressing room with people patting me on the back along the way. "Great show, man!"

"Thanks," I mutter, pulling my phone from my pocket and checking it again. Ben hasn't called me back after five calls and seven days. He and Ethan are tight but I'm not going to embarrass myself by asking for Ethan's help or any inside intel. Especially with Charlie due to pop any minute. I saw how she was when she interrupted our pool game nonstop – she's gotta be ten times worse now.

And after how I told my sister off I can't really give her a shout. *Yo, what's up with Ben and the girl I fucked over?*

Nevertheless she's all I can think about. Every night I'm dreaming of Paige. In Vancouver and Toronto I searched the audience for her secretly hoping she'd been nuts enough to stalk me and show up unannounced. How insane is that? I saw a girl in Montreal's airport when we arrived yesterday morning who from the back with a hint of profile showing could have been Paige. My heart nearly jumped out of my chest as I ran over.

It wasn't her.

The photo that girl asked me to take with her showed my disappointment.

These dreams are killing me. I can smell her in them. I can hear her begging me to fuck her. Feel the sting of the slap when I called her a bitch. And sometimes my salt-of-the-earth cousin is holding her in a passionate embrace, his eyes warning me that she's his. I've woken up in a damn sweat over both kinds.

Four of the dancers burst into my room a few minutes after the show, minus Olivia.

Jamilla is always their spokesman. "Gabriel, we aren't takin' no for an answer again! There is no way we are letting one more Canadian city slip by, with us on the dance floor and you in your fuckin' hotel room. Uh UH!"

"Ladies, I'm not in the mood."

"Is this because of Olivia? Because she wouldn't come when I told everyone I have had it with you moping around!"

I pop a top off a bottle of beer and mutter, "Nah, she and I are cool."

"Bullshit," Andrea says under her breath, brushing her long black hair with impatient fingers.

I flop onto the couch and throw a boot up as I motion to the door. "Go get her."

The dancers look at each other and Andrea bounds out of the room, producing Olivia a couple seconds later. She's not happy about it.

"You want something?"

"We good?"

She glances to the floor and crosses her arms. "Yeah."

"Hey, are we good or no?"

Meeting my eyes she stares at me. I hold her look with a small smile. Her pretty little lips start turning up. Then she relaxes and gives me a full-blown smile, releasing all the resentment in one decision to let it go. "Yeah, Gabriel, we're good."

I take a swig and slam it on the table. "Then let's dance."

Applause and dancing explodes from the girl and they're so practiced as a team that it looks choreographed. Proud of herself, Jamilla bounces over with some badass moves and throws an arm around my waist as I toss mine around her shoulders.

"I knew you wanted to get the fuck out of here. It's unhealthy, man!"

"Am I the poster boy for sane?"

We pass the roadies who are breaking down the stage.

They give me head nods and guy-waves – the subtle kind that show respect. These men travel with us, putting sets together, making sure our gear runs, loading it into trucks and the shit is heavy. They get paid okay but their motive isn't money. It's the music they care about. They get off being behind the scenes where it all goes down, building and breaking down the foundation for this entire glamorous creation. Just because they can't sing or don't play instruments, doesn't matter. Without them the show doesn't happen and they know that. But they don't socialize with us. The groups don't mix as an unspoken rule. It's like we're on two different planes.

But not tonight.

Louie and I lock eyes and I stop walking, my arm still casually around Jamilla. "Hey Louie, you and the guys come out with us."

He glances to the other roadies who are waiting for a verdict. One nods. All are surprised but men don't show it like women do, not when it comes to status and acting cool in front of other men.

"Yeah, we'll be there," Louie shrugs. "Soon as we're done here."

Jamilla says, "We're going to The Garage. Here's my number." She steps away from me and recites it as he thumbs it into his cell. He's a stocky Italian with dirt under his fingernails and she's a dark-skinned diva who loves her hoop earrings and manicures, but the look he gives her says something could spark between them tonight. And what a tornado of heat that's gonna be.

"I've gotta get showered," one of the roadies says behind us as Jamilla and I join the waiting dancers.

"How long does it take you to fuckin' shower? Shut up!" Louie grumbles.

Olivia holds my eyes, silently asking if I'm going to do anything else differently so she can prepare herself. The others break into a really bad rendition of one of my songs. As I check my phone one more fucking time, she gives up on me and walks with them.

How can none of these text messages be from Ben?

Pulling up Paige's number I stop walking and stare at it, thumb hovering over the call button.

Fuck it.

Just hit dial.

Press the damn button.

Jamilla calls out, "Gabriel, you coming? We want to get *drunk!*"

Shoving it in my pocket my footsteps pick up again. "Coming."

"My name is Paige and this is my first Al-Anon meeting."

Twenty-plus people seated in a circle at the Galano Club, say in unison, "Hi Paige." Some even add, "Welcome."

Tears slide down my cheeks. "I promised myself I wouldn't cry," I smile, wiping them away. The format of the meeting is structured with readings of the twelve steps and traditions in the beginning, plus some pamphlets telling the group that Al-Anon is for the family and friends of alcoholics, the sister program to AA. After the readings people share their stories focused on 'strength, experience and hope,' in three minute uninterrupted intervals.

The last fifteen minutes is reserved for newcomers to speak.

That's me.

I can't believe I raised my hand, but...I'm lost.

I need help.

"Um, my mother told me to come. She's a gambler not an alcoholic. But she told me the effects are the same and I heard someone speak about being raised with a rage-aholic so I guess it's okay for me to talk. God, I'm rambling, aren't I?" Several of the people smile with compassion. "When I was a little girl, she wouldn't come home for days. My dad – they're still together – he would hunt her down and make up excuses for why she'd left us. But I guess that gave me a feeling of abandonment early on. I'm the oldest child, so I took care of my brother through all of it. I was the mom. And then she found Gamblers Anonymous when we were teenagers and I thought everything was going to be okay, you know? You tell yourself that it's over. Even still, I've never healed from it. I feel tense in here all the time, like I'm all alone and have to do everything myself." I point to my chest. "Now it's happening all over again. My brother has disappeared again. This time he stole my jewelry. I finally called my mom and told her what I've been going through. God, I can't believe I'm crying like this." A total stranger hands me a tissue and returns to his seat. "Thank you. So, um, that's where I am. My brother is missing. I'm worried, but I'm always worried about him. The truth is I'm sick and tired of being sick and tired. I don't want to be a doormat anymore. He knows where to go if he wants to stop. Instead he took precious gifts my grandma gave me that I can never replace! I need help. If anyone has any ideas, please help me." Sniffling I whisper, "Thank you."

They always clap after every 'share' and the gentle applause for my desperate honesty is coupled with several voices quietly urging me, "Keep coming back."

When the meeting ends, a man says, "That's all the time we have. Will all who care to, please rise and say the Serenity Prayer with me?"

Everyone stands. The people to my left and right reach for my hand. One gives me a squeeze and I meet her kind eyes before she turns to recite a prayer I've heard my mother use, and never thought I'd say.

"God grant me the serenity to accept the things I cannot change. Courage to change the things I can. And Wisdom to know the difference."

The hands break from mine and friends starts chatting amongst themselves about the troubles and victories in their lives while others stack chairs and gather the reading materials.

An older, gay gentleman approaches with a gentle smile. "I used to be a gambler."

"You were? How did you stop?"

"I had to learn to stand on my own when my family stopped holding me up." He smiles at me, knowing that wasn't the answer I wanted, especially because I know it's true. "We're not allowed to give advice here. We can share our experiences and you'll take what you like and leave the rest."

"When they stopped helping, you gave up gambling right away?"

He shakes his head. "Wouldn't it be great if it was that easy? I had to hit bottom first. But I couldn't hit it when I was standing on their broken bodies." He spreads his hands out, miming a bridge. "When those were gone, I learned I had to change. Addiction is a cunning bastard. It lies. It's a bold-faced liar."

"I know," I croak, wiping my eyes.

He clasps my shoulder and says, "Keep coming back," before walking away to talk with other members.

Outside I walk into bright sunlight, squinting and running a hand through my hair as I wait for her voice, the cell held close to my ear.

"Paige?"

"Yeah, Mom. I just went to my first meeting."

She sighs with relief. "What'd you think?"

"Harsh wake up call."

A knowing chuckle comes through the phone. "I can imagine. What now?"

Staring at white clouds drifting in the sky I tell her, "I need to process everything, Mom."

"Your father might be someone you can talk to about this, too. He was where you are."

My stomach twists as I walk to my car. "I'll talk to him later."

"Please reach out if you need us."

We hang up and I immediately dial another number. "Ben?"

PAIGE

*R*eturning from the ladies room at Après Diem there's a bulletin board to my right that gives me a way to stall, so I pause. The only posters here are of local bands announcing shows at Terminal West and Eddie's Attic. These have the same style I've seen musicians use for years, but after meeting Gabriel and seeing what a real backstage looks like, they have more weight to me now. I can see the marketing behind the art. The mood they're trying to convey. And of course I wish I were looking at his face.

He hasn't called.

Not that he would.

Compacting the pain of my brother abandoning me, and Shelby not treating me the same as she used to, is the knowledge that Gabriel is on tour in all those amazing cities with Olivia in his bed.

My heart is ruptured.

And I'm leaning on Ben.

He's so grounded. Solid. Kind.

Here.

Forcing my feet to walk through the dark restaurant, the pastry display on my right, I see him at the bar patiently waiting. His profile is so familiar after we went through that intense night rescuing Shelby's money together. Heightened circumstances always bond people, but other than that feeling, my heart doesn't pump for him. Maybe it will in time.

"Hi, sorry, there was a line."

"Your crab cakes are getting cold," he smiles pushing the plate closer.

"You could have started without me," I smile back, picking up a fork. "These look delicious."

Ben adjusts his long legs and our knees touch. My fork freezes a moment before I drop it and carve out a small bite. I can sense that he wants to touch my hand, but since I've given him no sign I want him to, he's waiting.

Chewing in silence I blink at the memory of Gabriel pulling me out of Rays on The River and how good it felt when our fingers came together.

"This is yummy. Want some?"

"Sure." He takes a larger bite. "Mmm."

"Good, right?" We eat in silence for a bit and then I say, "Thank you for not bringing Bobby up."

"Figured you'd talk about him if you wanted to. How's Shelby?"

"Not good," I sigh meeting his eyes. "She shows up to work seconds before her classes and leaves as soon as they're over."

"That's rough. Have you tried talking to her?" I give him a look like that is a stupid question and he chuckles. "Sorry."

"I told her when she wants me I'm here. She didn't answer and I'm so sick of fighting stubborn people. I've decided that I have to take care of myself for once. Let's talk about something else. You have any brothers or sisters?"

Leaving the last bite of crab cake for me, he takes a gulp from his beer. "Only child. My parents tried but it turns out that when you hit perfection, God stops there."

Laughing, "Wow!" I finish off the food and smile, "Now I can see the relation!"

His sexy grin flickers at my bringing up Gabriel. To the bartender he calls over, "Can we get some french fries? Thanks."

I want so badly to ask about his cousin.

Have they talked?

Has Gabriel asked about me?

"So, um, are you close with your parents?"

"Yeah, they're the best. My Dad's like me, quiet. Mom was a travel writer, saw a lot of the world. She used to live in New York City."

"Oh yeah?"

"Yup, city girl in a country home," he laughs with

love in his eyes. "My dad's that good."

Laughing I hit his arm, "Don't talk about your parents' sex life like that!"

"Why not? Have you seen my family? Bunch of horny motherfuckers."

Cracking up, I shake my head, "I can't even imagine my parents doing it. No, scratch that. I don't want to! So gross."

Ben shrugs, "Sex is amazing. Everyone should be doing it."

My grin changes as he looks at me without hiding that he's thinking of us getting together. He's gorgeous, but it feels wrong to even think of it. I don't know if he is aware that I've already been with his cousin. He probably thinks I haven't, that I would not be the type who'd let that happen in the limo like I did.

Let it happen.

Who am I kidding.

I asked for it.

Begged.

God, I wish Gabriel was…

Raking my hair out of my face I stutter, "I, uh, haven't seen your whole family, by the way. So I have nothing to go on, but I'll take your word for it."

Ben smirks, "There are seventeen cousins in all, from six brothers. So that gives you a clue. It's in the genes. My grandfather was a stud."

"Oh he was, was he?"

"Definitely."

He holds my eyes until I become nervous again. "Are you the only one who doesn't have siblings?"

The french fries get placed in front of us and Ben asks for mustard. "My cousin Sofia Sol is an only child. We were born within months of each other, too, which is a weird coincidence since we're the only ones without brothers and sisters."

"Is she like you?"

Ben's eyebrows rise as he pictures her. "She is like nobody you will ever meet. Fearless. Fucking intense as hell. Independent in every way you could think of... except maybe when it comes to...Thank you." He takes the mustard from the bartender and doesn't finish his sentence.

"Except when it comes to what?" I smile, leaning forward and dying of curiosity. "I want to hear about the one thing she cares about."

Ben locks eyes with me. "Her family."

Leaning back my smile fades. "I know how she feels."

He nods. "Still don't want to talk about Bobby?"

"Definitely not," I mutter, scooping up french fries. "But I like hearing about you guys. Tell me more."

The rest of the dinner we spend with him sharing stories about his cousins, but Gabriel and his twin are left out in a pretty conspicuous way. I have a hard time believing they weren't there with everyone else at the ranch where most of Ben's memories take place. Finally I can't take it anymore.

"Where was Gabriel in all this?" His emerald eyes darken and he inhales like hearing the name is hard for him. "Aren't you guys close?"

"Yes," he admits, turning his beer bottle in circles as he stares at it. "But Elijah and Gabriel kept to themselves a little. Plus they were younger. The older cousins spent more time hanging out so we're closer. Just happened that way."

"Because they were twins, you think?" I'm dying to know more. The other stories were great but I can't deny that it's really Gabriel I've been longing to learn about. What am I, a masochist?

Ben shrugs, "Yeah, but we're still all close." He clears his throat, and looks at the bartender. "Can we get the check?"

"I'm sorry, I didn't mean to make you uncomfortable."

He smiles, drinks the last of his beer and lies through his perfect, white teeth. "You didn't."

Okay.

Huh.

Guess it's time to drop that subject.

GABRIEL

*L*ondon's fog drifting around centuries-old stone buildings makes me feel like I'm in a Charles Dickens novel here. All I need to take me back to that time is imagine the people in modern clothes are actually wearing top hats or elaborate Victorian dresses where little skin showed.

Like how modest Paige's lavender dress was...

Stop thinking about her, Gabriel.

You're losing your fucking mind.

I finally understand depression. Never felt this way, ever. Don't want to get out of bed. I'm roaming out here because the damn housekeeping lady's vacuum in the next hotel room kept reminding me the world is still moving.

I want this uneasy feeling to leave but since we flew in two days ago it's just gotten worse. My second concert here is tonight and we've got two more before flying to Ireland. I've got nowhere to be until tonight. I cancelled rehearsal because what's the point? We're a well-oiled machine, and I want to rest my voice. That's a fucking lie. I just don't feel like singing.

So I'm ambling around with no destination.

Just need a little distraction.

What's this here? A chocolate shop?

"You guys paint all these yourselves?" I ask the pink-haired teenager as I point to dozens of painted truffles that are laid out more like art than candy.

"Yep!"

"I'll take one of each. Make it two."

She nods and glances to the door as someone walks in. Her eyes narrow and dart to me. It's an odd reaction that causes me to look over.

My chest expands with shock and joy as I see my brother smiling at me in a long trench coat over his trademark black suit. "Elijah! No fuckin' way! What are you doin' here?"

He gives me a huge hug. "Surprise, Gabriel," he laughs in my ear as he smacks my back a few times.

We separate and I hold his shoulders, amazed I'm looking at him. This couldn't have happened at a better time. I needed to see him, and here he is. But I'm not going to say all that. He'd just give me a hard time for being a sensitive artist. We might look alike but inside we're polar opposites. "How did you find me?"

"Dad told me the hotel you were staying at. After I landed and checked in to surprise you, I put down my things and started walking. I turned that corner over there when I saw you pop in here. Guess my twin barometer still works."

I laugh, "No doubt!" To the pink haired girl I announce, "This is my brother."

She grins, "That's kind of obvious."

Elijah chuckles and points to the large foil bag she hands me. "Sweet tooth?"

As I dig out my wallet I explain, "Giving these to my band."

His eyebrows cock up. "You feeling okay?"

"Between you and Hannah you'd have me believe I'm a selfish isolated prick."

We walk onto the cobblestone street as my brother rubs his neatly trimmed hair. "Aren't you?"

Chuckling I admit, "Maybe I was but I'm done sharing the title with you."

He laughs, "Touché, fucker."

We get a lot of glances as we walk back to the five-star hotel, the longhaired rocker next to the stuffier mirror image. I was used to it when we were younger, but since it's been so long since Elijah and I have hung out I'm hyper-aware of how much we draw attention. It's weird though. Twins run in our family, sure but they're not uncommon in the world anymore. You'd think with all the fertility manipulations people would be used to seeing siblings like us. They aren't.

"How'd you get out of law school to come and see

me? You take the bar ahead of schedule and flip them off with your perfect score?"

He laughs, "I can guarantee you it will not be perfect. That test is a bitch I'm not ready for. But to answer your questions, finals happened. I told the Senator I needed to celebrate and take a couple days. Here I am. Also I heard from Ethan that you and Ben aren't talking."

I freeze in the middle of the street, and a horn honks at me. "Fuck you!" I shout at it. "Go around. There's more than enough room for your tin-can Euro piece of crap!"

Elijah frowns and motions for the guys to do what I said. As soon as the car veers around us, he locks eyes with me. "Guess I hit a nerve."

"Ben's talking about me but won't pick up a phone?" I bark. "I've called the bastard nearly every day, sometimes twice!"

My brother lays his hand on my shoulder and guides me to the sidewalk. His voice is lower than mine because he's used to caring what people think, unlike me. "Ethan says there's a girl. Which can't be true, is it? I figured he was nuts, but then I realized how far out of the loop I am with you." He holds my eyes. "I didn't like that at all, Gabriel. So I cancelled my calendar and got on the first plane."

"Does Dad know about the rift? Hell, does everyone?"

"He didn't say anything about it, which he would

have. And if he doesn't know then that means nobody does, except Ethan, Ben, me and you. Hannah would have definitely stepped in and called me, Dad and Mom. She didn't. So I think Ben's keeping it low, but what the fuck happened?"

"What did Dad say?"

"He just told me to hug you. Which I did so don't ask for another one."

I stare at him and chuckle after a second. "Keep making jokes. I need a sense of humor. Mine left."

His tone is flat as he shoves his hands into the pockets of his slacks, classic Cocker move when we're not pleased. "Who's the girl?"

"She won a date with me. Radio contest. I know, weird right?"

"Wow, your world and mine are so different it's insane."

"No shit," I mutter, raking my hair back as I spot a couple of girls taking photos of us from across the cobblestone street. "Get ready."

"For what?" he looks over as they run to us, giggling and looking a little high.

With a heavy British accent one gushes, "You're Gabriel Cocker, right? Is this your twin brother? It has to be!"

The other girl cries out with the same accent, "You guys look so much alike in person!"

Elijah and I glance to each other as I take the pen

and paper offered to me. Signing my name I hand it back and ask, "You coming tonight?"

"Tell me where and when!"

My brother snorts as I clarify, "To the concert."

She winks at me, "I know. Of course I'll be there. And anywhere else you want me to be."

"You guys have a good day now," I smirk with finality.

Overlapping they beg me, "Can we just have one picture with you?" "Yes, just one!" "Come on!" "Please!"

One photo turns into over thirty because the spectacle keeps drawing attention to the fact that I'm here and a crowd grows. A lot of people have driven into London from surrounding smaller towns to attend my concert, so it's not unusual for a number of them to be out shopping on this street.

When I'm finally able to break free, Elijah and I hurry our steps with our heads low.

"Jeezus," he mutters. "Have you really gotten this popular since the last show I saw?"

I throw him a look. "Maybe check social media every once in a while."

He opens the door for me to hide me from the populace. "I'm sorry, Gabes."

"Forget it. You're here now. This way." I guide him to a private lounge for V.I.P.s. As the heavy, wood door seals behind us, he and I head for the bar and order a couple glasses of Oban, neat. Nobody will bother us in here. The clientele are all millionaires of every kind. Old money. New wealth. Celebrity. Quiet owners of huge businesses whose faces you'd never know unless you read Forbes. They all come here for the privacy and exceptional atmosphere. No one is allowed who doesn't invest a ton of cash in the best rooms the hotel has to offer.

We settle into a couple, high-backed leathers chairs next to one of four roaring fires, agreeing that the strong burn of single malt Scotch feels so good sliding down our throats.

"Tell me about the girl."

"Can't stop thinking about her."

He pauses, surprised. "Why?"

"Who the fuck knows? I've been with how many women?"

Elijah smirks, "Don't tell me the number. I might get jealous."

"I don't even know the number. I've had three, four at a time, and you think that matters? Nope. Paige Miller...she's turned them to fucking dust, Elijah. It's messed up. She made my dick soft in Montreal."

His eyes narrow in an instant. "Come again?"

"Couldn't cum. That's the problem."

"Ha. Nice." He shakes his head at my stupid joke. "Explain, jackass, why you can't stop thinking about a girl who made you limp."

Chuckling to myself at my sophomoric humor I take a sip and set the glass on the marble end table beside me, the fire's heat warming my hand as it rests.

"Bunch of my team went out after the last show in Canada. Hooked up with some girl I met at the club, huge tits, French accent, super hot. We got to my hotel room, and I had nothing, man. Zip. Had to call a cab for her and reassure the poor thing it wasn't her fault over and over. Fucking nightmare."

My brother is staring at me. "This ever happened to you before?"

"What?! NO! You kidding? And don't look at me like it's contagious." After taking a gulp I mutter, "Couldn't stop wishing it was her with me and not that chick. She didn't kiss me like Paige. It was like I was kissing rubber, no sensation. Ever happened to you?"

He shakes his head. "What does this have to do with Ben?"

"He thinks he saw her first."

"Is she really that great? I'm having a hard time believing...I mean, I've never met anyone..."

Biting off the rest of his statement I say, "Yes, she's that great. She's grounded, loyal, smart, fun, everything you want in a woman."

Elijah smirks, "You didn't say beautiful."

"She's that, too."

"If you and Ben are fighting over her, I have no doubt she is. But I find in interesting that didn't top your list."

Staring at him a beat I think about it. "Guess the other things are more important."

"Because they last."

Setting my glass down I feel dizzy, like I've made the worst mistake of my life not running after her after that show. "Fuck. And you wanna know the truth? I knew it when I kissed her."

"Seriously?"

"I'm not even twenty-five, Elijah!"

"Oh really, I didn't know that."

"This is not a time for jokes!"

He exhales and fixes his gaze on the fire. "So you knew she was the one. You felt it in your gut."

"I felt it everywhere. I think I even said aloud that I wasn't ready."

"And now what are you thinking?"

"Ben's ready."

Elijah grunts and downs his Scotch. Rising up he motions for me to finish off my glass. I do, and hand it to him so he can get us another round.

Gold and red flames flicker across him as he stands above me and holds my look with a warning in his. "While I go refresh these bad boys I want you to picture one thing."

"What's that?"

"Our cousin inside *your* future wife."

Dynamite explodes in my chest.

PAIGE

alking with Ben through his garden I breathe in the sweet scent of organic strawberries. "It's so peaceful and beautiful here. I didn't realize how little time I've spent in nature lately, until now. They smell so good."

"You didn't answer the question."

Meeting Ben's concerned eyes I exhale and answer, "I have until the end of the month to vacate my apartment."

"Let me loan you the money."

Moved, I touch his hand. "I can't let you do that."

"I want to."

"I'm sorry, but I can't take a loan from you. I'm too proud, Ben. But thank you."

"Where are you going to go?"

"My parent's house for a little while. They're in Decatur so it's not that bad."

"Nice," he mutters, his mind working as he raises his gaze to the sun. "It's about noon. You ready for the lunch I promised you?"

"Mmhmm."

We head back to his modest home and again I sense that he wants to hold my hand. I lean down to pick a strawberry, to put a little space between us, hoping it's not too obvious how nervous I am.

I accepted his invitation knowing that today we'd probably kiss, since we didn't after dinner a couple nights ago. I'd avoided that, too. But I can't forever.

Watching him stroll through rows of fruit and vegetables I wonder why I'm still holding onto a man who doesn't want me when there's one right here who does. Ben is kind and attentive. His body is incredible. His smile, charming and sincere. He's so muscular, far more than Gabriel is, because Ben works on a farm. He built that shed over there! I mean, his shoulders are amazing, and the way those jeans fit, any girl would jump on his back and ride him all the way up to his bed.

So why do I feel sick?

This is wrong.

I have to go.

The sound of his phone vibrating causes both of us to look at his pocket as he checks it, and slides it away again.

"Who was that?"

"Nobody." But his eyes are troubled as he leads the

way up three steps to an open porch that's half complete. "I'm building this to be like the one my parents have. Our houses are different, Dad converted a barn, but I miss the enclosed porch. Figured I have the time to make it my own."

"Those are the best. My grandparents had one."

He holds the door open so I can enter his home first. Looking around I admire his simple décor. There's a lot of iron complementing pine and it needs a woman's touch, but it's homey.

"It's great, Ben."

"Let me give you a tour," he smiles, heading for stairs up ahead. I set my purse down on the coffee table and follow him up. "This is the first bedroom. I'm using it as guest room now for when my cousins visit."

Walking inside I run my fingertips along the goose down comforter. "I bet they love this in the winter."

He laughs, "You can't get Eric out of it!" Off my expression, Ben leads me out into the hall and explains, "He's a Quarterback for the Falcons. Let me guess, you don't watch sports or the news."

"Because I would have known who he was from his last name, huh."

"Exactly," Ben smirks. "Kinda hard to miss the name Cocker in this town. We're everywhere. Here's the guest bathroom." He doesn't pause to let me see it. "And here's my room."

I watch him enter without hesitation.

I really want to run back down those stairs.

But that would be extremely rude.

Walking in, I glance around a bedroom that is as comfortable as a teddy bear's tummy. His bed also has a goose down blanket, but it's king sized and adorned with eight feather pillows. There are two overstuffed, brown corduroy chairs by an empty fireplace, a round table between them that is just begging me to set a book on it so I can reach for some hot cocoa on a cool night.

He's pleased with my expression.

I glance to the master bathroom door and ask, "May I?"

He waves an arm, "Go right ahead."

"Look at this huge shower!" I cry out as I take in the stonework. "Did you do this?"

"I did," he smiles as he takes up the entire doorframe.

"These rooms are perfect."

"Glad you think so, Paige."

His tone hits me hard and I meet his eyes, seeing the change in him. This is the moment I could walk into his arms.

I could cuddle into him.

Forget I ever met Gabriel.

Forget all about Bobby.

Shelby.

I could just disappear into this farm.

Never go back.

Ben and I stare at each other. "Gosh, I'm hungry.

You?" I laugh as I squeeze by him and head for the stairs.

My phone is ringing.

Ben is walking behind me, but at a much slower pace like he's figured out this won't go the way he wants it to.

"Someone's calling," I lamely say, happy for a distraction. But a long, weird number on the screen makes no sense to me. "What's this?"

Narrowing his eyes, Ben says, "Europe."

"I don't know anyone there. Is it a scammer?"

The call goes to voicemail. Then his rings. He pulls it out and frowns at it.

My blood pumps faster as I realize what might be happening. He hasn't once called me so it didn't occur to me that it could be him, but now with the European phone number thing and the way Ben's frowning I ask the thing I'm most afraid to. Because what would this mean? "It's *Gabriel*, isn't it?"

On a sigh Ben nods and lets it go to voicemail, too. "Hey, I know he got under your skin but he's just a kid."

"He's my age."

In a move of stubbornness or ego, Ben pulls me to him and wraps me in his arms. Shocked I gaze up at him as he says, "He won't make you happy. I want you to give me a little more time here."

"Ben, I can't."

"Why not?"

"Because I'm wishing you were him."

He releases me like I stabbed him, backing away and running a hand through his sand-colored hair.

"Holy shit, ouch."

"I'm sorry, but it felt like you were about to kiss me and..."

"Wow. Just stop." He turns to the wall and lays his hands on it, head down.

"I'm sorry! I shouldn't have come here but…"

"Why did you?"

"I was weak I guess. And you're so strong."

"You're going to regret choosing Gabriel."

Anger flashes through my chest. "Don't talk about him like that. First of all you don't even know me. I think you're just looking for someone and I happened to be there at the right time. There's no way this was supposed to work between us because I don't feel that way about you. I just don't. So whatever you think is happening, it's misplaced." Picking up my purse I whisper, "Goodbye Ben."

He pushes off the wall to walk me out. I really wish he would've stayed there and stopped being such a gentleman. It would make this so much easier if he were a jerk.

As I walk outside I can feel him staring at me like he can't believe this is how our lunch date is ending.

Glancing back I offer an apologetic smile.

Tipping his head in goodbye, Ben crosses his arms and stands in the doorframe until I drive away.

PAIGE

 ow that I'm off his property, I breathe deeply to prepare myself for whatever Gabriel wants to say, and dial the strange number.

"Paige?!"

"It's me."

"Thank God."

"How are you, Gabriel?"

"Shitty, you?"

"Same."

"Because of me?"

"Not everything is about you."

He laughs, "God I love your fire."

"What do you want?"

He pauses a beat. "I need you to come to London. Also Ireland, Paris and Milan."

Speechless I pull the car onto the shoulder as gravel spits from under my tires. Yanking the manual emergency brake I stare at acres of bright green rolling fields outside my windshield. "What did you just say?"

"I said get your ass over here."

"I have a job. And..." Closing my eyes with embarrassment I confess, "I'm being evicted, Gabriel so I need to work."

Without missing a beat he snaps, "Quit and get another job when you get home! Aren't there other yoga studios you could work at? They're on every corner of the city."

"I guess so but I...still have to pay rent."

"No buts. I need you here. It can't wait. I'll buy you a first class ticket. You can get another job when you return and I'll front you some money for the rent."

"No way! I won't accept it!"

Gabriel mutters a couple cuss words, then, "Don't go away. I'm putting you on hold and calling Maggie."

The phone goes quiet. Just when I start worrying that he's forgotten about me again, Gabriel's beautiful voice comes through. "You there?"

I whisper like speaking too loudly will make me wake up, "I'm here."

"Carrie has an apartment you can stay in until you get on your feet. She's always at Maggie's anyway. They're not ready to move in but they...anyway, problem solved. I'm going to book the flight. How fast can you get to the airport?"

"Is this really happening?"

"Yes, it's fucking happening! Now how long?"

"Um...I'm not in Atlanta."

"Where are you?"

I mutter, "North of it," not wanting to say.

"Are you at Ben's?"

Wincing I confess, "Yes."

"Dammit shit motherfucker sonofabitch! Elijah, she's with him! Paige, listen to me. I know Ben is more mature than I am and you have that yoga shit in common but I'm begging you, give me a chance. I fucked up by not chasing after you. I know that. I was freaked. I don't deserve this but please give it to me anyway. Give me a shot. Please come to London."

In shock I blink and whisper, "Okay."

"Yeah?! You'll come?"

"Is this really happening?"

"You just asked me that!"

"Is it?"

He laughs, "Yes! Elijah, she doesn't think I'm for real. Am I for real?"

I hear a voice that sounds like his call out from the distance, "He's for real!"

"Believe me now? How fast can you get to the damn airport?"

A smile sneaks out from my heart. "I'm an hour from the city. I have to change and pack."

"I'll buy you clothes."

"No, I'm in a short-sleeved blouse and shorts. It's hot here. I can't fly on a plane like this – they're like ice in the sky."

He pauses, "Okay. I'm just…desperate. Do what you have to. Keep your phone on and charged. I'll call you back with possible times and we'll figure this out together."

Together.

God, sounds so good.

PAIGE

*L*ondon's airport is like any in America regarding security – if you don't have a ticket you have to wait in designated areas. When I get my baggage and have passed through customs I am free to join the rest of the world.

My breath hitches as I see Gabriel and his twin brother. He's searching and doesn't see me yet. When our eyes lock his light up on a grin. He holds up a handwritten sign like what chauffeurs use when they're picking up people they don't know.

His reads in a messy manly scrawl, all capitals: *BEAUTIFUL PAIGE* .

I melt…until he flips it over to read: LUCKIEST CONTEST WINNER EVER.

Cracking up I make him laugh, too. Elijah watches with guarded interest as Gabriel and I hug.

"You're here," he rasps in my ear. "I couldn't stop thinking about you."

Tingles spread down my body. We pull away, smiling at each other.

He laughs, "You're supposed to say the same thing."

"You were kind of a jerk. I'm still not sure what to think."

His head bounces to the side and back. "That's fair. And I bet Ben kept you busy."

His brother warns, "Gabriel," as they lock eyes. He offers his hand. "I'm Elijah. Nice to meet you, Paige."

Taking in their similarities and differences I smile, "Nice to meet you, too, Elijah."

Gabriel explains, taking my hand, "We have to get back to the hotel. I have one last show tonight in London before we head to Ireland tomorrow."

Our fingers entwine as though it's natural for them to be like this, but I'm nervous. And jet-lagged. Seeing that dancer again isn't my idea of fun.

I flew out last night, but with the ten hours it took to get here, plus the time difference you can't argue with, it will be way too soon that I'll be forced to see them onstage, with her gyrating all over him again.

"I didn't know you had a concert tonight."

"I didn't tell you that? I guess there was so much to organize I assumed you knew. It's why I'm here."

"Of course."

Elijah is rolling my suitcase, one hand in his pocket, his stroll casual and confident. We meet eyes and he gives me a smile. Gabriel's energy is more loose and wild. His brother feels cold and distant. I bet his home is immaculate and if anything is out of place he loses his temper. I wouldn't be surprised if he confessed to firing a dozen maids, that's how Type-A he seems.

A black luxury sedan is waiting for us and the driver takes my bag and stores it in the trunk as Gabriel helps me in and slides in next to me. Elijah climbs in with the same grace his twin has, and takes the seat opposite us. His pale green eyes don't have the rogue splash of amber. They're sharp and intense even as he leans back and separates his legs in a casual way. "So, Paige, you took a big leap."

Biting my bottom lip I glance to our hands as Gabriel increases his grip. Meeting his eyes I see encouragement there and it's baffling. What was the big change? How did this happen?

"My life is a little crazy right now so I figured why not go full gonzo?"

Elijah grins. "You're our age right?"

"I'm twenty-three."

"Close enough."

"But I'm the oldest child so I've always been more..." I pause, feeling silly.

"Gabriel called you grounded."

Glancing to my right I ask, "You did?"

He nods as his thumb caresses mine. "Yeah."

"That's a nice thing to say. But I don't feel it lately. I feel...in control of nothing."

They subtly nod at the same time, and Elijah glances to the window as we put the airport behind us. "That's what the most enlightened minds of the world say is the correct way to view life. We are in control of nothing except for our reactions to what happens to us."

I add, "And those reactions then create a ripple effect throughout."

"It's a lot of pressure," he murmurs, still staring out like the world's problems are his to solve.

Gabriel explains, "My brother is going into politics like our father. Won't be surprised if I see him in the White House one day."

"Really?"

Elijah meets my eyes. "That's the goal."

"What will you do when you get there?"

"I'll tell you then," he winks.

"That's assuming we'll still know each other."

The twins share a mysterious look and Gabriel kisses the side of my head in the sexiest way. He holds there and whispers, "Can't wait to get you alone."

My lips part on a tummy clench. Subconsciously I glance to the watchful brother and clear my throat. I know he heard that. Suddenly I can imagine what I hadn't even dreamed of before – that they've shared women in bed. The idea is tantalizing but there's no way I'm made for that. I tend to bond; it's in my nature.

Now that I'm in Gabriel's presence again I know that's why I couldn't bring myself to touch Ben much less kiss him, why it felt wrong. It was because this feels so right.

But Elijah scares me a little. He feels cold.

"Wow, you want to be President."

Gabriel asks, "You know our dad was a Senator, right?"

My stomach turns over. How did I forget all about what Justin Cocker did for my brother? My voice gets smaller as I say, "Of course. Right. I knew that."

Gabriel presses his lips to my fingertips. "Don't worry about him. He's a good guy. Little stiff like Elijah is, but heart of gold."

"Gold that's kept locked inside Fort Knox," Elijah dryly says, rolling his eyes to the window again. "Dad's harder to crack than I am."

"You trying to scare her off?" Gabriel laughs.

"I'm just prepping her for reality."

"Well, cut it out, fucker." He looks at me. "My mom is the one you won't be able to live without. He married up when he chose her."

I'm staring at Gabriel, stunned at the words he's using, like it's a given that I'll meet his family.

What is going on here?

Biting my lips I just nod and give an awkward smile.

This makes the sexy jerk laugh. "Look at your face!"

Elijah chuckles, "Can you blame her? You're laying it on thick and fast, Gabes. She just got here. You jet-lagged, Paige?" I nod and he motions, "See? She's not in

London twenty minutes and you're saying she's going to love Mom. You've lost your fucking mind."

Gabriel shrugs, unbothered. "When I know what I want, I don't fuck around." He kisses my hair again and says, "I want you."

My mouth slackens and I glance away, staring out the window and feeling like I might faint. I've stopped breathing. He puts gentle pressure on my hand to get me to look at him again. Swallowing both fear and hope I meet his eyes.

"I'm serious, Paige. I want you."

Glancing to his brother for confirmation that this is real, I get no smile or hint of amusement to indicate they're messing with me. Elijah is gazing at me like it's just a fact.

The car turns right and Gabriel leans to peer out the windows. "We're here."

GABRIEL

*W*e leave the stage with the encore still saved up, and I stroll to where Paige and my brother are standing. I had her backstage this time to watch from the sidelines with him rather than from the mosh pit. Could have done that in Atlanta but I was running then. Tonight I wanted her close.

With bright eyes she says, "That was so great!"

"You think so?"

"Yeah," she grins.

It occurs to me that she's relieved Olivia and I don't have that choreographed number together anymore. I ditched that before Montreal. Probably could have let her know before the show started, but all of this is new to me.

Elijah agrees, "Better than last night, too. Think you might have had an effect on him."

Paige's cheeks flush as behind me the crowd is screaming for an encore. My band motions to me and I nod. "I'll be back."

We head out and finish the show. Knowing she's here and watching me is a high. As the final song ends I tear off my shirt, throwing it into the audience as they lose their shit. The band ends with drums banging a sexual beat and then slamming to a close. Feeling better than I ever have I raise my arms and shout to the crowd, spiking the mic and walking offstage.

The curtains roll shut and the dancers bounce toward the three of us, fist bumping me as they go. Olivia glances between Paige and I and offers her a conciliatory smile before vanishing with the others into the main green room where the party happens.

We go to my dressing room. Glancing to Elijah, who knows the story, I give him a look. He catches on and says, "Great show, Gabes. I've got a date with a front desk clerk."

My eyebrows cock in surprise outside my door. "When did that happen?"

"When I checked in." He starts to head away and decides to confess on a smirk, "Oh, and she stayed in my room last night. I don't tell you everything."

"You tell me nothing!" I call after him.

"Almost true," he chuckles, holding his hand up as a stationary wave. "See you at breakfast before our flights."

Paige is chewing on her lip again as I rest my hand on the small of her back and guide her inside. She's in a tighter dress than the one she wore in Atlanta and while she looks hot as hell I know the reason. As soon as I shut the door I pull her to me. "I'm a little sweaty."

She smiles, "And yet oddly you still smell good to me."

"Chemistry."

"Mmm," she hums, long eyelashes falling to my lips.

"I didn't have sex with Olivia after the concert."

Her eyes sprint up. "You didn't? But I saw you zipping…"

"She'd started to strip and she unzipped me before I had a chance to tell her we weren't doing that anymore."

Paige searches me for the truth. "So you used to."

"We did, yeah. But that stopped when I met you."

"Why?"

Without hesitating I shrug a shoulder. "Couldn't get it up for anyone else after that."

Her beautiful eyes blink in surprise. "Really?"

"Swear to God," I smirk. "And trust me, no guy likes to admit when his cock goes limp."

A grin flashes on her as she presses a quick, soft kiss to my lips. "Gabriel, I didn't touch Ben. Not once. No holding hands even."

My gut tightens. "No kissing? Nothing?"

She shakes her head, holding my eyes to show she's

telling the truth. "Nothing. I did spend some time with him. I was trying to forget you, because it seemed like you didn't care about me at all. And…this is hard to say, but he did care. I've been going through a lot of stuff that you don't know about and I was…grasping for some kindness."

"I'm such a fuckin' idiot," I groan, pressing our foreheads together.

Her hands travel up my arms. "I just want to take it slow though, okay?"

"What's been going on in your life? What did he help you with? I swear I want to kick his ass right now. And he didn't even touch you."

She smiles like I'm the strangest creature she's ever seen, and maybe I am. But men become protective when we find the woman who is meant to be ours. I didn't know that until it happened to me.

"Can we talk about that later? You just did an amazing thing out there. This is your night and I just want to be here with you."

She has no idea how much 'my night' this really is now that she's here. I crush her body to mine and kiss her without hesitation. She responds as if she was dying to be closer to me, too, and just like the first kiss outside her apartment, I hear a click inside my soul. I lift her up and her legs hook around me as our jaws unlock, tongues tasting each other like they never thought they would again. Moaning I carry her to a wall and let my hands roam where they want. She's clutching onto me, her breasts crushed into my naked chest. "This dress is too sexy. I have to get it off you," I rasp.

She laughs, "Who's stopping you?"

Grinning I gaze into her eyes as my fingers slip under the tight hem and slide across her G-string. "Damp as fuck. I can't believe you're here." Dipping under the wet fabric I feel her pussy and groan, "Why weren't you in Canada?"

Her eyes close as she smiles, "Because someone didn't invite me."

"Someone should have." I slam my tongue in her throat at the same time I slip my middle finger in her tight little cunt. "You're sopping wet, baby."

"I want you," she moans. "I can't believe I'm here with you, Gabriel."

Our mouths reach for each other as I grind against her thigh and thrust another digit in. The sounds she's making are driving me crazy.

The door opens and Maggie pokes her head in, sees us, says, "Whoopsie! Oh, Paige, you're here! Eek. Goodbye!"

Paige's eyes go wide with embarrassment. I give her a quick kiss, don't stop finger-fucking her, and say, "We just gave her spank material."

Paige laughs and then starts moaning as her pussy clamps a couple swift beats around my fingers. "I'm going to cum."

"Do it!"

"No, I want it to be with you, when you're inside me." As I raise my eyebrows she grins and gives me what I want to hear. "You're going to make me say it, aren't you?"

"Mmhmm."

She moans as I tease her pussy, and then murmurs against my panting mouth, "I want your cock, Gabriel. Your gorgeous cock needs to be inside me right now. What the fuck, did I fly all this way for nothing?"

Grinning I hike her whole body higher up against the wall, her legs now on my waist so I can get these leather pants out of the way. It's impossible to get them all the way off in this position and who the fuck cares. Hotter to have them hanging halfway down because we're too impatient. Pulling her thong to the side I kiss her as my thick, bulbous tip starts to penetrate her. "God, you're so tight. So wet."

Paige cranes her hips to give me better access and the moan that vibrates our joined mouths ricochets. We lock eyes and she looks scared. "I've never felt like this, Gabriel. My heart is pounding too hard."

"Mine too."

"Please don't be toying with me."

Shaking my head I hold still in the deepest point in her. "I'm going to show you I meant everything I said."

My body takes over and she yields to me. We're panting and fucking against the wall, breaking free from hungry kisses to watch each other, then crashing our mouths together as the time we spent apart disappears.

As she whimpers in my arms I tell her, "You're mine and I'm never letting you go."

PAIGE

With our hair damp from the shower, I'm lying on Gabriel's chest in the King Size bed of this beautiful, five star hotel suite, blankets and six-hundred-count sheets bunched to the side, away from our naked bodies. He's playing with a lock of my hair as I tell him about my brother, the Al-Anon meetings, my mother and her history. The questions he's asked have been thoughtful but not overly concerned about how this impacts him.

"A lot of people would be shocked by what I'm telling you."

He smiles, "Musicians see a lot of dark things, Beautiful. Nothing you're saying is worse than what I've seen on the road. And the dark side of life inspires my music. Can't sing about rainbows and happiness all day. Nobody would listen to it because life isn't like that."

"I guess you're right."

"We'll get along better if you memorize that sentence."

I stare at him a second and start laughing. "Oh no, I will be the one who is right in all arguments from here on out."

He chuckles, "So you left even though you don't know where he is? From what you told me that seems like a big step. Should I be flattered?"

I smile at his making light of it, and trace one of his nipples, giving it a quick kiss before I lay my head on his warm chest. "Bobby has to make a decision. He needs to ask for help. I can't let him hurt me anymore." Meeting Gabriel's eyes I say, "This last time, you know what he said? That he was going to the gym. When he didn't come back I checked my jewelry box for the millionth time and my fears finally came true."

"Your brother stole from you?"

"Yeah." I lay my head back down, finding comfort in the steady, quiet thumping of his heartbeat. "That's when I knew he wasn't coming back soon, if ever. That he'd stooped that low meant he was really gone. Wouldn't be able to face me until he could pay me back and that won't happen while he gambles."

Stroking my head, Gabriel murmurs, "I'm sorry."

Mustering up courage I rise up on my elbow. "I have to tell you something."

"What is it?" he frowns.

"It might be the ending of us."

Gabriel laughs, "And we've only just begun."

"I'm serious. When I came here I didn't know you were thinking long-term things, and...well, I didn't know what you wanted when we talked on the phone yesterday. Everything happened so quickly and I had just told Ben I wasn't interested. So my head wasn't clear. I didn't remember until in the car after you picked me up at the airport."

"Okay, go ahead. It can't be that bad. As long as you didn't lie about not hooking up with my cousin."

"No! It's not that! I haven't lied."

"Then what is it?"

"Your father knows about my brother. I met him. Ben called him to find out where illegal poker games were taking place."

A frown springs to Gabriel's face. "What?"

"I guess he has connections with the police department and they know about these things but let them slide as long as they're contained."

"No, I'm aware of how he knew where to look. Was he there?"

"Yes, he and Ben helped extricate Bobby from the game, and get his money back."

Gabriel rakes his fingers through his hair, pushing it up on the pillow. "Shit."

"I should have told you when I remembered, but I didn't know how. Especially with Elijah there and then when you told me about Olivia and we attacked each other..."

"No, it's fine. We'll deal with it but…" Gabriel closes his eyes, wincing. "I can't believe that's how you first met him. That's how he sees you."

I rise up and bring my knees to my chest.

Gabriel sits up, too. "He hates addiction, Paige. My Uncle Jason, his twin, was infatuated with this ex-model named Bernie when he was younger. She was a big cokehead. Dad watched his brother almost go down with her."

"Oh no," I whisper.

Gabriel rubs his face. "Yeah, uphill battle already. Fuck." I move out of his way so he can throw his legs over the side of the bed and walk to the bathroom, shutting the door as my heart closes in on itself. I'm not so good with abandonment. I want to chase him and knock on that door.

Pulling the covers over me I lie down and wait for him to return. It's taking forever and my knuckles are white.

When he finally walks back he's still naked, which to me is better than if he'd reemerged with a towel on. That would have felt closed off. But his eyes are shadowy as he glances my way several times as he paces.

Crawling on all fours he returns to me and pulls the blanket and sheet back. "No no no, I need you naked," he murmurs before kissing and laying on top of me, his soft hair hanging down and blocking the view of anything but him. Deep and troubled he explains, "I'm trying to think of how to handle this. The problem is I'm sort of the black sheep of the family. Hannah kind of led the way in our house and Elijah and I tagged along, kind of. But Elijah...he's the golden boy now that he's following Dad's path. They have that in common. And Dad's really close to Hannah because of what happened when she was a kid. That leaves me on the outside."

"You don't feel you have his ear or patience."

Gabriel relaxes, "You get it. Thank you."

"I wish my brother wasn't an addict, or my mom, but I can't change it. If you want to take back what you said, I understand."

"Shhh, don't get upset. It's all good. If anything we can travel the world together and never have to see my Dad or your brother." He makes a funny face that makes me smile. "That's better. We'll figure it out." Flipping us over so that I'm on him again he closes his eyes and caresses my shoulder as he whispers, "Have to get some sleep. I'm glad you're with me. This bed needed you."

Pulling up the covers I nuzzle into him. "If you change your mind and can't do this because of your Dad I will forgive you."

Gabriel's finger and thumb cups my chin to make me look at him. "Paige, I'm keeping you with me, and if he doesn't like it, that's tough." He kisses me tenderly, holding my body to his. We settle back to cuddling, him on his back and my head tucked into him.

"If I wake up in Atlanta tomorrow, I won't be surprised."

Gabriel's sleepy voice is fading fast. "If this is a dream then that would be the nightmare."

Smiling I murmur, "This is why you write songs and I don't."

His chest rumbles on a tired chuckle. A second later his breathing shifts and I know he's sleeping. How he can do that after we've talked about something so serious is a mystery I long to unravel. And I spend over an hour trying to figure it out.

GABRIEL

*I*n the V.I.P. Lounge, Paige and I find Elijah waiting in one of the chairs near the fireplace again, his suitcase to his left.

"How'd your night go?" I ask him.

Looking at our clasped hands he smirks, "Not as good as yours, but she was fun."

"Have you seen Maggie?"

"She just left to check you out of the hotel you lazy bastard."

Paige and I sit on the couch facing the flames, leaving the other chair empty. "You're just jealous because you do the grunt-work for your Senator."

"Paying dues," he shrugs. "We all have to. Remember the dirty room you played at Smith's Olde Bar on Monroe?"

Laughing under my breath I mutter, "They gave us six bucks each for that gig."

"High roller," he smirks then glances to Paige. "You look rested. My brother sleep the night away?"

She rolls her eyes. "I'm not answering."

"So that's a no," he dryly smiles.

"I won't take the bait," she says.

Kissing her head I whisper loud enough for Elijah to hear, "Tell him he's an asshole."

"No!" she laughs and waits a comedic beat. "He already knows."

My twin and I crack up. She looks pretty proud of herself, but what she doesn't know is how much that kind of humor will fit into our fucked-up family. Too many arrogant bastards to go around – male and female alike. None of us were taught humility, if the meaning of that word is to make yourself small so that others don't hate you. Fuck that shit. My father always said, *It's lonely at the top but loneliness never felt so good.*

At the airport Elijah and I say our goodbyes since we're on different carriers, the gates on opposite sides of the terminal. I give him a bear hug and whisper in his ear, "I'm really glad you were here to witness the beginning of this."

He pulls away, rare emotion in his eyes as he clasps my shoulder and says a sincere, "Me too, Gabriel." As Paige hugs him he kisses her head. "Take care of my best friend for me."

"I will," she smiles.

He strolls off in yet another black suit, matching carry-on suitcase gliding along the tile just behind him.

"Elijah!" I call out.

He pauses. "Yeah?"

"I love you."

A smile flashes on him. "I love you, too."

Roping my fingers with Paige's we head for our gate and I tell her under my breath, "He wears black suits because they look better on him than Dad, since Dad's blonde and black washes him out. He likes peacocking around in black Armani."

"Really?"

"Don't tell him I told you."

She laughs. "I'll save it for ammo."

"That's my girl."

We've checked our bags so our arms are swinging as we walk and I feel light on the inside. Glancing over I find her smiling, too. "You happy you're here?"

"Mmhmm. That was really sweet with you guys. Couple of Alphas showing they care. Awwww…"

I bump my hip into hers. "Hey, don't make fun of us."

"But you're so adorable. I love you, Elijah! Muah muah muah!"

A burst of my laughter inspires people to look at us. I've got sunglasses on and a baseball hat, but I don't feel like calling attention to myself. Shutting it down I whisper in her ear, "You're hilarious, you know that? Now cut it out."

She grins, looking ahead. "I like the sound of your laugh too much. Prepare to be fucked with."

"Oh, I'll prepare to fuck alright."

"That's not what I meant and you know it!"

Tickling her I keep my voice quiet as I warn her, "You won't win this game."

"I will, too!"

She squeals as I dig into a tender part of her waist. Again people look over. We clamp our mouths shut and keep walking, but we're trying not to laugh.

As the gate comes into view so does my band, roadies and dancers. The groupies don't fly with us. They find us somehow, though. We never know who tips them off, but several of the same girls showing up at every city we play in. My suspicion is that they pay one of the roadies off for the intel, but I've never been able to get a confession out of anyone.

Maggie walks up to us sucking iced-latte through a straw, shades on her eyes, too, and her dark curls wild and smelling of shampoo. "When did I miss this memo, huh?"

"Carrie didn't tell you Paige is staying at her pad after she gets back to the ATL?"

Maggie pulls her sunglasses up and stares at me. "What the fuck. You serious? Excuse me." She heads away to make the call.

Paige and I stay off to the side of the gate, with her leaning against a wall and me facing her, the public behind me. "I never asked you about that ankle tattoo."

Smiling she says, "It's fire and water."

"I saw that. What does it mean?"

"Balance. I got it when I was eighteen and thought seriously about teaching yoga." She's gazing up at me and brushes my hair from my eyes. "Olivia still likes you."

"I know."

"Are you really over her?"

"I was never under her…in a manner of speaking."

Paige winces and glances to my lips. "I can tell you want to kiss me, but don't in front of her."

"I can do whatever I want."

"Gabriel, I want to be kind."

I lean in and give her a quick kiss. "I'm not going to full on make out in front of her, but I do want everyone here to know how I feel about you."

Paige stares at me with surprise. "Oh."

"When I said you're mine, I meant it. That wasn't just the heat of the sex, talking. I'm claiming you, Beautiful. Especially with how bendy you are, Jeezus. I've got a hot yoga chick."

She hits my chest, "Oh shut up."

Laughing I glance over to the dancers and see Jamilla and her crew watching us, but Olivia is facing the windows. I give her a head nod and Jamilla returns it. It's as good as written in cement now. I'm taken and a new chapter has begun for me and that means for the band, too. Whoever wants to stick around is welcome to as long as nobody fucks with my girl.

I've fallen for Dublin, how charming it is. The people are so warm, their accents fun to listen to. Many of the younger girls here wish they were tan so they wear foundation makeup a shade darker than their pale skin that rarely sees the sun. Lots of blue or purple eyeliner and hip fashions taken from the London runways twisted into their own personal style like they one-upped the system. We've been here four days and it's been absolute bliss.

"I think I'm crazy about the Irish," I confess to Gabriel as we walk into a pub built in the 1700's. "Did you hear that bartender call that drunk guy an eejit?"

Working his way through the late-night crowd, he explains, "It's idiot with an accent."

"So funny!"

"In London they call everyone cunt. In America you can't get away with that shit. But that's because it doesn't mean the same thing. To the Brits it just means you're stupid. Or a douchebag."

Rising on my tiptoes I urge him ever-so-quietly, "You can use that word with me in private, though."

He cocks an eyebrow at me. "Oh yeah? Noted." After pressing a quick kiss to my lips he turns and tells the ginger-haired bartender, "Two Guinness."

Squeals coming from the far end of the dark pub make us both look over. Gabriel's been spotted by a group of female fans. Bowing out I tell him, "I'm going to the ladies room. Have fun."

He gives me a nod and turns to accept their praise and request for autographs and photos. I overhear them giggle that they were at the concert tonight and can't believe he's here. This happens everywhere we go. Price I have to pay, I guess. I've discovered the trick is to separate the star from the man. I get the man, they get the star. But the star is untouchable so I win.

Steep, narrow stairs lead me to the second floor where exaggerated conversations are taking place across mismatching tables and old wooden chairs.

A sign on the wall points left and reads: Toilets.

And of course there's a line. As I take my place, my hair falls over my face while I dig for my lipstick. I don't see I'm standing by Olivia until I hear her say, "Funny how they call them Toilets here, huh?"

Looking up on a smile I'm about to agree when I freeze. "Oh um, yeah." She's much prettier close up, which of course drives my mind to horrible images in an instant. I'll never forget what her boobs look like. How I wish I could.

She rolls her eyes, acting friendly, "In the states we're so puritanical we have to call it a Restroom."

"When nobody is resting in them, ever."

"Right?" she smirks while glancing down to the lipstick in my hand. "I have that color. That's Blushing Berry, right?"

I read the label quickly because I have several shades from this brand. "Yep. What a coincidence," I mutter.

We're silent as the line moves forward one.

She leans her back on the wall and bites her bottom lip. "So that's the second thing you and I have shared."

I stare at her profile. "Okay, just say what you've gotta say."

She eyes me, the friendly façade gone. "Why you? Why not me, huh?" She pauses, getting angrier. "Why didn't Gabriel pick me? We've been hooking up for over a year and yeah, it was casual, but I kept thinking that one day it wouldn't be! I thought we'd wake up and he'd still be in my bed for once, not run off like I was trying to sneak some ball and chain around his fuckin' ankle." We have a growing audience now but she does not care. "This whole time I tiptoed around his fuckin' ego thinking he was just scared, but that wasn't it at all! He wasn't into me. He didn't give a shit this entire time!"

I want to crawl into a hole and hide. "If it was going on for a year, he must have felt something."

She shakes her head, wagging her finger like she doesn't want to hear it. "No. Uh uh, when I see him with you he's proud and letting everybody know that you're his girl."

My mouth opens and shuts.

She waves her hand in the air indicating the whole group of them at the airport the other morning. "He did that to show *me*. To make it really fuckin' clear that it is done, over, and I'm supposed to do nothing and act like it never happened. Do you know how shitty that feels?"

All I can do is shake my head.

Gabriel has discovered us and works his way through the crowd. "Olivia, that's enough!"

She turns on him, "It happened! I'm a human being and you were in my body over and over!"

"Oh Jeezus," he mutters. "You want to talk about this, we'll talk. But not out here in public." He grabs someone's phone to stop them from videoing. "Keep it up and you're gone."

She starts laughing in his face. "I fuckin' quit! How 'bout that!"

I glance around as photos and videos are taken so quickly he can't do anything about it. It feels like the entire bar has surrounded us by how condensed these faces are.

Olivia goes on, "Get yourself a better dancer and

good luck because one doesn't exist! You trade me for her? Ms. Tiny Tits here? You fuckin' crazy?" She pushes my shoulder.

I don't know if it's the fact that acting like a coward would be recorded for all eternity, or that between my brother and my upbringing I've had enough of taking people's abuse. Whatever the reason, my fist hits Olivia's face so hard her head spins and she falls into the wall.

Gabriel's eyes go from ferocious to shocked.

Cameras are still aimed at me.

But I can't see them anymore.

All I see is this bitch losing her dignity and trying to take me and Gabriel down with her.

Wide-eyed she stares as I demand, "Who do you think you're talking to? Check yourself Olivia, because I will knock you down again if you ever breathe on me, understand? You don't love him because you wouldn't be making this scene like a child. You loved the idea of being with him. But I *do* love him. And there can be only one."

I take Gabriel's hand and together we push our way out of the crowd to freedom. He takes the lead to negotiate these steep fucking stairs that are crowded with curious faces and cameras. "Out of the way!"

On the cobblestone streets of downtown Dublin we hurry past closed shops to put space between those cameras and us.

When they decide to leave us alone and the voices

fading behind us become silent, Gabriel pulls us into a shadowy corner and takes my face in his hands. "Wow."

Throwing myself into his arms I kiss him and whisper, "That just slipped out. It's too soon! I didn't mean to say it. I didn't even know I was going to!"

Searching my eyes his voice is thick as he tells me, "Hey, Paige, stop. I love you, too."

Melting into him I whisper, "You do?"

He kisses me roughly and I respond with equal excitement. Gabriel pulls away to say on an amused smirk, "Remind me never to piss you off."

PAIGE

I hold my forefinger and thumb an inch apart. "I thought you were a *little* off key during *Can't Wait Campaign*."

Gabriel snorts as we stroll through the rolling hills and sunny tree-lined paths of Parc des Buttes Chaumont in Paris. "You do, huh? Hate to break it to you but you're wrong."

Struggling to hide my smile I insist, "Seriously, right in the middle of the song there was this teensie weensie little moment that wasn't absolutely without a doubt perfect like the rest of the show. I was appalled. I don't know how you look in the mirror."

He grabs a pink blossom from a bush we pass, and smells it. "If only I had someone to give this flower to who wasn't overly critical."

While looking at the sky I smile, "If only."

He backs up to set it where he found it. "Oh well."

"Give me that!"

Holding it out of reach my gorgeous man fakes innocence really, really well. "What...this? You want this? Grab it from me then."

Shaking my head on a grin I head away. "Nope. Don't need it."

He hurries after me, behaving like a commedia dell'arte character, twirling an invisible mustache. "Oh? Why not?"

Spinning around I slip my arms around him and look up into his eyes. "Because I have you and that's all I need."

His pale green eyes flicker and change moods instantly. He sensually cups my head and whispers, "One minute I'm giving my cousin Ethan shit for getting married, and the next I've got images of you walking around my loft with a ring on your finger and my child in your arms."

My heart skips while I stare at Gabriel, speechless as the sun dances across his skin like Mother Nature is licking him.

We kiss and let the Parisians around us disappear. I feel the flower pressed into my hand as we separate. "I might have bent it."

"It's beautiful." I smell the crumpled petals. "No smell though. Try harder next time."

He bursts out laughing, shaking his head. "Oh we're going to get along fine."

Our fingers lace as we walk further. "You know I'm messing with you, right? I think you're wonderful, Gabriel."

From the corners of his eyes he holds my look. "I know. Don't worry, Gorgeous. I've got siblings and cousins with the same sense of humor and it just means love. If we're not giving each other shit then something is wrong."

"My brother and I didn't do this," I quietly say. "But in our house there wasn't a lot of fun and playfulness growing up."

"You want to call and check on him?"

A long, painful breath leaves my lungs. "No."

"You didn't tell me how you handled your apartment before you flew over to be with me."

"*To be with you* — that sounds so good."

We stop for a fashionably dressed couple pushing their baby boy in a stroller. "Bonjour," the man says with a polite dip of his head.

"Bonjour," we reply. The woman nods to me as they move along. They don't recognize Gabriel, which just adds to our relaxing afternoon.

After a few steps when we can't be overheard, I explain, "My mom was so happy I was finally doing something for myself that she and Dad packed up my apartment for me." Off Gabriel's curious expression I explain, "I thought they'd turned their back on Bobby when they wouldn't let him live there anymore, but really they turned their back on enabling him. She knew I had to find my own way. They call it hitting bottom, where there's nowhere to go but up. I had to get to that point, myself, before they'd help me. Seems harsh huh?"

"Nope. You had to ask for help," Gabriel mutters. "What's harsh is your brother stealing from you. That's gotta kill him as much as it hurts you. I think when you stopped allowing it he might have been relieved. Like you're telling his demons no more. It'll give him the strength to tell them to fuck off, too, when he's ready."

Staring ahead I let that idea soak into me. "Wait, explain."

"If he's in there, in the dark corners of his mind fighting these demons...wait. First let's say they're not imaginary, that they're as real as you and me and they are loud. If that's true then when people allow him to do what the demons tell him to do, it almost gives their direction credibility. But when enough people in his life, especially the ones who matter most, say, *no more,* he's then forced to look at the demons and ask himself why the fuck he's listening to them. And he can make a choice."

"You think he couldn't make the choice before?"

"I think it's harder." Gabriel rakes a hand through his hair and stops walking. "We used to have a different drummer, a guy I knew from childhood who gradually disappeared into drinking. It inches up on you. He didn't see it coming. Neither did we until he started fucking up, not showing, missing rehearsals and finally a show, and then another. We loved the guy but had no choice but to let him go the night we had an audience of two hundred waiting for us to go on, and no drummer."

"Oh no. What did you do?"

"Luckily the band who opened for us was still there and it was a fucking miracle because their drummer was a fan. He'd seen all of our garage shows and little dives and shit. He knew most of the songs and we improvised. It was crazy." Gabriel smiles with disbelief because it still amazes him how lucky they were. "We kept him and that's when things skyrocketed. His old band was fucking bummed but what are you gonna do?"

I went to two meetings before I got Gabriel's call. As we walk across the suspension bridge this park is known for I tell him, "When I get back to Atlanta I'm going to get a sponsor and see if I can't…I don't know. I'm still trying to grasp how it all works."

Gabriel nods. "They have sponsors in Al-Anon?"

"Yeah. I'd like to have a guide. Mom can't do it. It can't be family, especially not your qualifier. Anyway," I smile, squeezing his hand to get back to what he asked me. "Mom's storing my car in their garage, and they boxed up my clothes. The furniture is being donated to the women's shelter on Howell Mill, because Carrie's place is furnished and she said I could stay as long as I like. When I get my own place I want to start over with things that don't remind me of the past. It's just stuff. I want a fresh start. I'm going real 'minimalist.' Only buy what I need as time goes on. Doesn't that sound amazing?"

A thoughtful grin plays on his handsome face. "Nah, I like to carry a ton of crap with me wherever I go."

Hitting his chest I laugh, "Your suitcase is half the size of mine!"

"That's to impress you when really I'm carrying around eleven clunkers they have to stow in every hotel. Even have a couple cats in them."

"You're a mobile hoarder, is that it?"

"One of my suitcases is just empty takeout containers."

"Stop. Do I hear another waterfall?"

"This is where I wanted to take you." He points to a slice in the small mountain just up ahead.

"Is that a cave?" I gasp, excited and tugging his hand.

"Yeah, it's a grotto."

"What is that?"

"Just means it's manmade. They even formed these stalactites, look. Those aren't real."

Staring up at the limestone spikes reaching for us from the moss-green ceiling I can't stop smiling. "It's beautiful here."

"This waterfall was manmade, too."

He takes my hand and walks us as close as we can get, where the spray cools our skin. In between kisses I lock eyes with him. "This reminds me of something Ben said."

He cocks an eyebrow. "Oh?"

"The mill doesn't have a waterfall. It's a dam."

He dryly asks, "Is water falling from it?"

"Yes."

"Is it bigger than this rinky-dink thing?"

"So much bigger."

"Then Ben doesn't know what he's talking about."

"Who's Ben?"

Gabriel laughs. "That's better."

I show him my flower. "But you gave me this pretty little thing so it's all okay."

"Oh, and I'm a flower-crusher, too."

"Nobody's perfect."

He looks me dead in the eye and smirks, "Wrong. I'm perfect."

I cry out, "Oh my God, you're so ridiculously cocky!"

"Nobody in my family has ever been called that before."

I stare at him. "Really?"

He laughs, "No, not really."

Rolling my eyes I slip my fingers into his belt loops and give a tug. "You think we could have sex in here and not get caught?"

"Want to spend the night in a foreign prison?"

"Maybe?"

Two children who can't be more than six years old run in, their high pitched voices unabated as they race each other. Their tourist parents appear, looking around with long oohs and ahhs.

Gabriel whispers in my ear, "Let's try it."

I push him away and start walking out, shaking my head.

GABRIEL

I can't get close enough to this girl.

It's the first time I've been on stage and was distracted, looking forward to when I had her alone again. Never been in love before but holding her in my arms as she sleeps is better than eating.

She's dreaming. I can tell it's not a good one so I kiss her forehead and whisper, "It's okay, babe, I've got you."

Her eyelashes flutter open and bleary eyes focus on me. She burrows closer and murmurs into my neck, "Thank you."

"Any time." I close my eyes and get ready to let sleep take me out but her hand stretches out on my abs and begins to travel downward. "You're that awake huh?" I smile as she slides her soft open palm over my growing length.

"Mmhmm." Nibbling my earlobe she murmurs, "I love your cock, Gabriel."

"Something every guy wants to hear," I groan as she strokes me. I'm filling up more by the second, an ache beginning in my groin.

"Every guy wants to be called Gabriel?"

I laugh and stretch my hips up, gently fisting her hair and guiding her to kiss me. "C'mere smartass." Her deep brown eyes are hooded and lusty before our mouths find each other. She gives the base of my shaft a tug and then glides a firm hold up my length. It's so good I moan into her lips, "Keep doing that."

"You like it?"

"It's perfect."

Her smooth leg slides over my thigh. She's on her side, me on my back hard as a rock. Paige's tongue plays with mine and I feel a steady pulse build in my core. My hands find her hips and I lift her up to mount me. She loops the other leg over and cages me in with her hands on either side of my head, her long hair creating a cave around our faces as she lowers her sweet pussy onto my tip. We're gazing at each other as I penetrate her and rasp, "You're so wet."

She licks my lips and whispers thickly, "I love touching you. Stroking you." She kisses me then murmurs, "Making you want to cum before you even get inside my cunt."

Laughing in surprise at her word choice I tease her, "Yeah? Getting dirtier, huh, Paige?"

"You're a bad influence," she smirks, rising up as I hit her cervix. I reach for her breasts and rub my thumbs over her nipples in little circles as she toys with my erection, keeping the in and outs short when she knows I want to go deep every time.

"You're teasing me," I groan, craning my hips. But she keeps control and adjusts rising with me.

"Ah ah ah," she moans, adjusting again and riding me in short bursts that are driving me crazy with desire. She dips down so that I'm all the way up in her, and holds there. I grab her hips to start pumping with thick strokes but she grabs my hands and pins them back. I could fight her but this is too fucking hot. Her hard tits are held by gravity as she keeps my hands over my head and rides me in short bursts before slamming one down to completion, then more little bursts, then all the way in again.

"So good," I groan closing my eyes on a grimace of hunger for more. "God you're so wet."

We kiss as she moves a little faster, her moans as contained as her moves. Suddenly I feel like I'm going to blow so I break from her kiss and lock eyes with her. "Fuck baby, I'm almost there."

"Me too," she moans, eyelashes half-mast. She begins to move and says, "Take over!"

I don't need to be told twice. I grab her hips and grind my cock all the way into her, enjoying every second of watching her receive me. She grinds a little and I lose my shit. "Oh fuck!" I groan, fucking her harder until her pussy starts to palpitate against me, pulling my orgasm with each tight grip of hers. I roar and thicken, shooting my hot juices in her until I have nothing left.

She falls onto my chest and kisses my face as I gasp for air. In soft caresses her lips travel to my earlobe and give it a final nibble before she murmurs, "You're mine."

Out of breath I hold her soft body closer and turn my head to kiss her and whisper, "Promise?"

*C*arrie explains as she points to it, "Hot and cold are labeled wrong in my shower. If you need it warmer turn the knob left not right."

"Got it. Thank you for this."

She waves my gratitude away. "I'm never here. Glad someone is using it. And you're helping me out, paying half the rent."

"I can pay all of it soon."

"Oh no, then it would be like I'm really living with Mags and I'm not ready for that yet." Walking out of the bathroom she gestures to a cupboard we pass. "Towels and sheets live here. We met while I was living with another woman, one I'd moved in with *way* too quickly. You know the old joke right? What does a lesbian bring on her second date? A U-Haul truck." Carrie rolls her eyes as I laugh. "It's funny because it's true. So I told Mags, don't even bring up us living together for at least two years."

"How long has it been?"

"One year three months three days."

"You're counting."

She smiles, "Don't look at me like that. Your phone is ringing."

I hurry over to the kitchen counter and dig it out of my purse. "Hey Mom. You got my message saying I'm back?"

"Your brother contacted us."

My heart skips as I walk into the living room and motion to Carrie that this is important and I'll be right back. "Is he okay?"

"He's still in it, hon. He wanted to come over but he sounded jittery. When I asked if he was still gambling he wouldn't answer me, acted like he didn't know what I was talking about. I firmly told him, *Bobby, I love you. You are welcome here as soon as you get clean and we can trust you. It's completely up to you when that will be.*"

"What did he say?"

Mom sighs, "He called me a bitch."

"Oh no!"

"He's fighting it, but honey, these are the last stages."

"What if he never comes out?"

"I'm afraid that's his choice, not yours. He saw my recovery. Bobby knows what he can do when he finally surrenders, more than most people."

Closing my eyes at how hard this is to say, I whisper, "Please don't tell Bobby where I am."

Mom's voice is heavy. "I can only imagine him gutting your friend's home for what he can sell."

"I don't want to even think like that but I have to. I'm so torn though. Like if he knows I'm here then he'll reach out and take my hand."

"How long did you hold it out?"

Sighing I admit, "Two years."

"And did he take it?"

"No."

"I had you kids at home, my very own children, and I still disappeared for weeks. It wasn't until the locks were changed and I was told I couldn't return or see my family that the veil lifted and I finally realized I had a real problem."

"I didn't know Dad changed the locks!"

"He kept you in the dark on purpose, Paige. You and Bobby had been through so much. You don't know it, but things got really nasty for a while. Anyway, your friend is waiting for you. But I have to know, how was the trip?"

I smile at the soothing reminder of Gabriel. "We had a great time, Mom. We were in Milan for just three days and it was so industrial that he rented a car and drove us to Verona so we could be somewhere more romantic." Pausing I tell her, "I feel safe with him. He looks out for me."

"When can we meet this fancy musician person?"

Chuckling I tell her, "Soon. We're getting to know each other. I need to find a job. Just let me get settled, okay?"

"Take your time. I should probably listen to some of his music, too, so I don't come off as some old lady who's out of touch!"

"You're not old. I have to go. Thank you for storing everything for me and making that trip possible. I love you, Mom."

A surprised pause on her end makes me realize I haven't said that in a long time. Filled with emotion she says, "I love you too, Paige. Talk soon."

After we hang up I don't move for a few seconds, and whisper, "Wow!"

Carrie's head pokes into view from inside the kitchen. "That was the sweetest thing I've ever heard."

"Eavesdropper!"

She leans on the doorway, head tilted. "I lost my mom when I was eighteen to cancer."

"I'm so sorry."

Her eyelashes dip toward the floor. "We all have hard stuff to go through, I guess."

I walk over to give her a big hug, pulling away to ask, "Can we be friends, like real friends?"

With a huge smile she says, "Mags and I were saying that we hoped we'd be friends with you!"

"You did?" I laugh. "Really?"

"Anyone who will go along with that crazy scheme

we made up to hide the fact that you and Gabriel banged it out in a car on the first date, is okay by us."

Covering my face I crack up. "Oh my God! I think I love you!"

On a wink she says, "Don't tell my girlfriend that. Now let me show you the garage because the light switch isn't where it should be."

"Charlie's in labor! Get your ass to the hospital!" Ethan shouts before the line goes dead.

Adrenaline shoots through me as I stare at the phone, excited for him and also noting that he called me himself, didn't activate the family's phone vine. In a situation like this, our version of a phone tree would definitely be the way to go. So I've gotta admit – I feel special right now. He wanted to tell me himself. I wonder if Hannah told him I feel left out where the older cousins are concerned.

Calling Paige I wait for her sweet voice to answer. Seems like it takes forever but that's because I'm dying to get to that hospital.

"Well hello there, Handsome," she says with an audible smile.

"Hey Beautiful, you still with Carrie?"

"She just left."

"I'm coming over to pick you up. My keys are already in my hand and I'm heading out the door right now. My cousin's having the baby!"

I told her about everyone while we were traveling. We had a lot of hours in the day and I know for a fact I overwhelmed her, but she impresses me by remembering his name. "Ethan and his wife? Oh my God!" She pauses, losing the happiness. "Wait, do you think it's a good idea that I go with you?"

"Why not?" I mutter, locking up. "Oh shit, I didn't think about my dad." Raking a hand through my hair I look up at the blue sky and feel like nothing can go wrong today. "Fuck it. This is a big day in our family's lives and I'm not leaving you out of it."

"That's so sweet, but Gabriel…"

"Don't argue with me. What did I say to memorize?"

"Something about you being right all the time."

Jumping in my purple Audi I mutter, "Never forget it."

A chuckle disguised as a cough comes through the phone before she says, in forced seriousness, "Got it memorized…Gabriel Cocker is always right. All the time. With everything. No exceptions."

As my Audi purrs to life I smirk, "Keep it up. You're making me hard."

Breaking into laughter she can't hide anymore Paige says, "Your ego could power this whole block."

"What are you talking about, block? The whole fucking city! I'll see you in minutes."

As soon as we hang up I call Ben, but drop the call before the first ring. At least I hope it didn't go through. Fuck, I really want to hear his side of what went down with Dad and Paige so I can mentally prepare myself for this. But Ben still hasn't called me back so this isn't the time to ask for advice. Fucking asshole. How long is he going to let this go on?

Growling I dial my brother. "Hey, Elijah, Ethan call you?"

"No, Emma did. You heading to the hospital?"

Surprised Elijah got the phone-vine treatment I say, "On my way there now."

"I'm in D.C. and will fly out tonight."

"Dammit," I mutter, seeing a yellow light and going through as it turns red. A guy honks at me and I flip him off and yell, "Fuck you!"

Elijah laughs, "I'll get there as soon as I can, jeez."

Frowning despite his joke I explain my situation, "Dad's met Paige already and not in a good way. I don't know what to do. Her brother has a gambling problem that Dad stepped in to fix."

"How'd that happen?!" Elijah barks. He knows full well how our Dad feels about that shit.

"Ben called him when he was trying to get in Paige's pants. How do I handle this?"

Elijah is silent as he thinks about it. Then he exhales loudly. "You're bringing her to the hospital, aren't you? You're too fucking stubborn to keep her at home and introduce her at a better time."

"Have her miss something this important to the family? Fuck that!"

"Gabriel..."

"No, you don't get it, man. I was like you. Remember how much grief I gave Ethan when he knocked up Charlie? A fucking billionaire wants to settle down when he can get all the pussy in the world? Remember I told him that?!"

"Yes," my brother groans, impatient and imagining the worst with our father meeting Paige under the circumstances we're in.

"I couldn't understand why he would do that, Elijah, but I get it now. You'll see when you find your girl. Something happens in you. She's a part of me now and I'm not leaving her out of this important day. Dad will just have to deal with that."

"No, you'll have to deal with Dad, but whatever," he grumbles. "And don't tell me how it's going to be for me, okay? You don't know what you're talking about. Marriage is good for Ethan, Hannah, Ben, you. I know Emma is dying to settle down if she can only find a guy who doesn't bore the shit out of her. I've no doubt Eric will get married and have like eight little jocks. But me and Sofia, we aren't like you guys."

"Keep telling yourself that," I mutter as I pull up to Carrie's single-story house.

His voice is dark and annoyed as he says, "I know who I am, Gabriel. It's you who didn't know who you were. Ya think you weren't destined for one woman? I always knew you'd go that route. You're like Uncle Jason! An artist with your heart on your sleeve! You couldn't write those sappy fucking songs that make girls cream their panties if you weren't a hopeless fucking romantic. You mean that shit when you sing it. It's not an act. I'm like Dad. You can't go into politics and be soft. If Hannah hadn't come into his life then he and Mom wouldn't have made it. And that lightning won't strike twice. I'm going to be the first President this country has ever voted into office without a wife, you watch."

Paige appears in the doorway wearing white jeans, ballet flats and a silk, lavender blouse. Staring at her from inside my car I tell my jaded brother, "My girl is walking toward me right now, and if you could feel what I do as I'm looking at her, you wouldn't fight this so hard. I've gotta go."

"Tell her I said hello."

"You got it."

Hanging up I jump out to open the door for her. She steps into my arms and kisses me. "I'm nervous."

"I'm not going to let anything happen to you."

She gently laughs. "You make it sound like your Dad might attack me."

Kissing her nose I open the door and guide her in. "My brother just gave me some speech about how he's never going to love anyone."

"Really?"

I make quick strides to the other side, swooping in

and shutting the well-designed door with a quiet click. As we pull away from the curb I explain, "He's saying I'm the romantic one like our Uncle Jason and *he's* like Dad. Which is ridiculous."

"Didn't you say Jason is a musician?"

"Music producer. It's not the same thing." I glance to Paige as she cocks an eyebrow. "It's not! They're behind the music. Listen to this." I reach for the volume and tell her, "This is a rap album he produced a decade ago. You think this sounds fluffy?"

Paige argues, "I'm sure Elijah didn't call your music fluffy!"

The passenger window shatters, glass flying.

Our airbags explode.

I grab Paige's hand as her body bends toward mine.

The Audi flies left.

It slams into another car.

Everything goes dark.

GABRIEL

here the fuck am I?
My head is pounding.

Blinking at the ceiling I see one cold, fluorescent light fly by. Then another. And another. A woman's face appears, long black hair flowing as she runs by my side.

"Gabriel! Who am I? Do you know who I am?"

Touching the wetness draped in pain on my forehead I moan, "Mom?"

"Oh thank God," she whispers.

I hear Dad's voice shouting, "No photographs! Someone keep these people away from my son!" A pause then, "Jaxson! Jason! Jake! Thank God! Help me get these bastards out of here!"

"Where am I?" I rasp as her fingers tighten on mine. "Is this a dream, Mom?"

"No, honey, you've been in a accident."

My memory hits me as I jackknife up. "Where's Paige?!"

"Gabriel, shhh, lay down! You're bleeding really badly. You need to stay still!"

Two doctors fight me as I shout, "PAIGE! PAIGE!!!"

My dad pushes them back and holds me by my shoulders. "Listen to me! Calm the fuck down! You are hurt!"

I give in and let him push me down onto the gurney as it turns into a sterile room. Scrubs tell my parents they have to leave but I call out over their patient voices, "Dad! Where is she? Is she dead?"

"She's in surgery."

"Who is Paige, Justin?" Mom asks, confused and scared for me.

The door closes and a mask is put over my mouth as I hear him say, "Just a girl."

Everything goes dark again.

PAIGE

"Hey," Bobby chokes, holding my hand.

From under the weight of medication I blink at him. "Bobby? Where are we?"

"You've been in an accident. The hospital called me. I'm your emergency contact on your insurance... ironic, huh?" Tears jump to his eyes. "I thought you were going to die!"

Mom and Dad appear in the doorway behind him. From the looks on their already worried faces they didn't know he was here. I shake my head a little to let her know not to do anything about it. It's so good to see them all together.

I rasp, trying to understand what's happened, "My throat..."

Bobby glances to our parents and explains it to them as much as to me, "Glass from the window cut you. It just missed your jugular. They stitched it up...

your head and arm, too. You broke two ribs." He wilts onto my hand, bent over as his shoulders shake.

Dad rests a calming hand on his back.

Mom comes to the other side of my bed, lovingly pushing matted hair from my cheek. "We came as soon as the Senator called."

The memory of the accident slams into my drugged haze. "Gabriel," I choke, terrified.

Dad says, "I don't know if you still call him Senator when he's no longer in office."

"Oh who cares," Mom mutters.

"GABRIEL! Is he…"

"He's alive," Bobby says, gripping my hand tightly to reassure me. "He's okay, but the hospital is surrounded with fans and reporters. His family has gotten into some fights with them, protecting him. It's crazy out there."

"What they made us go through to prove we were your parents," Mom mutters.

"I need to see him!" I try to get up but Mom and Bobby hold me back. "Let me go! I need to see him!"

"Can you give us a minute?" a deep voice says. We all look over to find Justin Cocker standing in the doorway, his jaw tight. "I'd like to talk to Paige alone."

My dad doesn't like the look on his face and, just like he was argumentative about calling Mr. Cocker a Senator, his spine protectively straightens again. "Why do you need to? How'd you know our number anyway?"

"Stephen!" Mom cries out.

But Dad isn't going to let her steamroll him this time. He locks eyes with her. "Elaine, Paige is hurt and this guy doesn't look friendly to me." He turns to Mr. Cocker and snaps, "I'm sure you're used to getting your way but I'm not letting you near my daughter until I know more about you, understand?"

Ice-green eyes narrow as Mr. Cocker slides his hands into his suit pockets. He's about to speak when a beautiful, older, raven-haired woman appears and touches his shoulder with love. She must be Gabriel's mom. That's where he got the striking dark hair and that brown streak in his eye. "Justin, what are you doing?"

He glances to her. "Jaimes…"

"No," she gently whispers, squeezing his hand and grazing over my parents and brother before settling on me. She walks passed her husband. "I'm Jaimie Cocker. You must be Paige," she smiles, and glances to my family. "And you are?"

They each introduce themselves and shake her hand. It obvious she's a politician's wife because her poise stills the room.

I can't stop staring at her. I've heard so many wonderful things about his parents and seeing them here without Gabriel by my side brings so many emotions in me that tears are sliding down my cheeks because I feel it all coming to an end. "Please don't tear us apart," I whisper before I even know I'm doing it.

Mrs. Cocker's face contorts with emotion. Bobby lets go of my hand and steps aside so she can stand closer to me because she wordlessly told him this is where she needs to be. Gentle fingers float down to rest on mine. "Sweet, sweet girl, I wouldn't do that to my son."

Mom is blindsided. "Paige, why would Mrs. Cocker try to do that? I'm sorry, but I don't understand what's going on."

Bobby chokes, "Because of me, Mom." He crashes out of the room and Mr. Cocker has to step aside to let him go.

Realizing that they haven't been told everything, my father demands, "What is going on!?"

Mr. Cocker exhales like he doesn't want to do this, but will anyway. "I bailed your son out of a bad situation. I'm not sure if you know about his gambling addiction."

Dad looks at Mom, but doesn't betray her secret. She's paid enough. "We know."

"He stole a debit card from Paige's friend and we got the money back, but it was a dangerous situation for everyone as you can imagine. I thought she was dating my nephew, not my son. I don't want…"

Mrs. Cocker interrupts him, "What my husband is worried about is the mental and financial well being of our son. I'm sorry to be so blunt, but you are intelligent people and you can see he's upset. I don't want you struggling to guess why. It's better to simply talk about these things. I wasn't raised in the South where everything is underlying and unspoken. In Boston we say what's on our minds. I think that's best so that everyone is aware what we're dealing with and can get past it."

Mom defensively snaps, "Paige should not be punished for her brother's problems. She's a sweetheart who has never done anything illegal in her life!"

Dad adds, "There is no better girl than my daughter!"

Mrs. Cocker inhales and touches her husband's arm. "This is not because of Paige, I assure you. My husband's brother was romantically involved with an addict once upon a time. If my son loves Paige, and it was made very plain to me today that he does, then I'm sure she is wonderful and I can't wait to get to know her better, and all of you. This is my husband's issue that he needs to see an analyst about."

"Jaimie!"

"You do, honey. It's time to let what happened with Jason and Bernie go. No two situations are alike and you are acting like they are."

He glares at her, turns on his heel and leaves the room.

My father growls under his breath, "If he says a bad word about Paige I will personally kick his teeth in. Excuse me, I have to go find my son!"

He charges out of the room.

That's the nicest thing my father has ever said.

GABRIEL

*C*racking my eyes open I see my sister and brother beside my hospital bed. Hannah gasps as Elijah runs a relieved hand down his face and groans, "You're awake."

"Where's Paige," I rasp. "Tell me she's alive. I need…"

"She's okay," he says.

Hannah glances between us and adds while touching her neck. "She got cut up pretty badly but they had a plastic surgeon in to do the stitches. The driver had all the right insurance so that's good. They should heal well." Taking my hand, my sister whispers, "I didn't know you were in love. Why didn't you tell me? After our fight, I should have called."

"Elijah told you," I hoarsely whisper.

"Yes! But I wish it had come from you. I know it's

my fault. I've been…not great in the whole older sister department." She drops her head and caresses my wrist. "I guess you're not my 'little brother' anymore, huh? Guess I have to start thinking of you as a man."

"Duh," I smile, making her look me in the eye. "I tried to tell you that in Florida."

"I know."

We squeeze each other's fingers as I glance to Elijah and ask, "Ethan's baby?"

"She was born 'bout an hour ago. They named her Kaya Marie Cocker."

"Pretty."

He nods and adds, "Dad and Mom are fighting about your girlfriend."

Closing my eyes I grimace at the image. "Doesn't fucking surprise me in the slightest. Go get her."

"Mom?"

"Paige, you idiot. I need to see her."

Elijah smirks. "I'm glad the truck didn't rob you of your charming personality."

"Or my life!" I smirk back. "I need more pain meds, too. How big was the thing?"

"Just a huge fucking truck. Not a semi, or you wouldn't be here. I'll see what I can do about getting your girl here." He rakes determined fingers trough his hair, the other hand in his suit pocket as he strolls out of the room.

Hannah sighs and motions to dozens of elaborate

flower arrangements stuffed into this small space. "Word got out."

"How bad is it?"

"Uncle Jaxson is in jail. Uncle Jake beat up some paparazzi guy and crushed his extremely expensive equipment but since it's Ethan's child being born Uncle Jaxson told the police it was him. Clearly he wanted Jake to see the birth of his granddaughter! The photographer argued but when the cops heard, 'Why would I want to go to jail? I broke the fucking camera!' they took Uncle Jaxson away. Dad's working on getting him out by tonight. Especially since he told them to do it."

"Laughing hurts," I grin. "Try to be less funny. Anyone else get in trouble for me?"

Ethan strolls in with a swaddled bundle in his arms. "Yeah, me. You stole my thunder you narcissist." He twists to show me a sleeping baby girl whose tiny fingers are resting on the pink, fuzzy blanket. "Look what I made all by myself?"

Hannah laughs at his joke piggybacking on the narcissist comment, but I'm staring at the creature like the miracle she is. I can't believe I want one of these now — that's the miracle. "Give her to me."

"Not a chance. She has to stay clear of germs and you're a fucking mess, Gabriel. You get cleaned up and we'll talk. I just wanted to show you, and make sure you're okay." He heads out, cooing to his daughter, "Your second cousin is an attention hog, Kaya Marie, so he went and got hit by a truck today. Yes, he did!"

Mom walks in, her gaze resting a moment on watching Ethan as a father. She turns her head and holds out her hand. I reach for it and our fingers squeeze. "Gabriel, you scared me. Don't do that again. I'm going first, you understand?"

"Mom, don't even talk about that."

She kisses my forehead and whispers against it. "I love you so much it's not even funny."

"I love you, too."

Straightening up she and Hannah share a look like this was not fun for either of them. Inhaling sharply to change the subject, Mom stiffly smiles, "Your father is angry with me. Did your brother and sister tell you what happened?"

"They said enough and I already knew it was going to be hard. He doesn't like Paige."

"He doesn't *know* Paige!" she grumbles, pushing her long hair back. "But I met her, and she's just adorable, honey."

"She's fucking beautiful, is what she is."

Hannah laughs and shakes her head with Mom mirroring her.

My Uncle Jason, dad's twin, sticks his head in the room. "How's it going in here?" He glances around and sees it's just the three of us. Locking eyes with me he strolls in wearing grey jeans and a blue, cotton, long sleeved shirt. Aunt Sarah, his much shorter wife turns the corner, pushing curly red hair from her face, wearing a dress that matches his shirt.

"Gabriel! You look like shit!"

"You gotta stop sugar coating things, Aunt Sarah."

Since he mixes all my albums, Uncle Jason and I have that bond. We always talk business so he asks, "How was the tour?"

"Sold out in every city. Canada was hard. London got better...when I had company." I hold his look with meaning.

His eyes narrow and he glances to Mom and Hannah since my comment was purposefully mysterious. "What's this? Your boy meet someone?"

Mom smiles, "Yes. Maybe you can help us."

"With what?"

"If Dad wants to be stubborn, let him!"

She touches my arm. "Don't get upset. You need rest."

My aunt and uncle are very interested in finding out what happened. Mom explains it to them as Hannah and I watch and wait. We're expecting Uncle Jason to offer a solution but it's Aunt Sarah who gives the key. "Well, that's ridiculous. What does he think, that it's contagious? Every family I've ever known has an addict or alcoholic in it. Look at my brother Nathan!"

Jason and Mom stare at her as the realization dawns on them. I know Nathan but not well. He lives in Detroit so we didn't see him much at family functions over the years, but since he owns a comic book chain we loved it when he came to visit. He always brought all the best graphic novels, even showing us which ones were going to be huge before they hit big.

Hannah takes the words right out of my mouth. "I didn't know Nathan ever had a problem."

Uncle Jason mutters, "Excuse me. I'm going to find Justin."

JUSTIN COCKER

I'm pacing outside, in one of those small under-furnished courtyards that can only be accessed from inside the hospital. No paparazzi here and nobody to bug me. Except Jason as he calls out, "There you are! I've been looking for you everywhere."

"Don't tell me my wife sent you to calm me down."

Jason crosses his arms, eyeing me. "She did, actually."

We are still the mirror image of each other, my twin and I. Our hair has gone grey in the same way, solely at our temples. We've both stayed trim because our egos have kept our gym memberships paid up and used to their advantage. Our eyes, unlike my twin sons, are identical.

But Jason has always been a softie.

Playful.

Optimistic.

Me? Not so much.

"You don't know the whole story," I grumble. "I saw that kid when he was at the table, and afterward he was like a dog trying to get back in to finish a dried out bone. He had an out. We were there to save him. And he didn't want it."

"Sometimes it gets really bad before it gets better," Jason says. "Not every time, but that's how it is for some."

"I don't want Gabriel to have this in his life. That kid will always be a problem. He'll want money. He'll suck their time. And what about their kids?"

Jason's eyebrows go up. "Are you saying my children are going to be addicts? Which one, Lexi? Samantha? Can't be Max, he's too wise. Maybe Caden? Hunter?"

Staring at him I make an annoyed face. "What the fuck are you talking about? Of course not! You didn't marry Bernie!"

"I married Sarah whose brother was a heroin addict." Jason pointedly looks at me, knowing I'd forgotten all about who Nathan used to be. I met him when he was clean — never thought twice about it after that. "We are talking about Paige's *brother*, too, aren't we? Just like my wife's brother?"

Running a hand over my hair I pace away from him. "It's not the same thing."

"How is it not? Heroin is worse, isn't it? More of a social stigma."

"Nathan got clean!"

"So might Paige's brother. Bernie finally got clean and you never thought she would. She teaches third grade now and has a family of her own. Would you condemn her today?"

Completely out of proportion to our discussion I explode, "Jason, I'm sick of your looking out for them! When are you going to learn?!"

He stares at me, dropping his arms and shoving his hands into his pockets. "You're still pissed at me. Jaimie's right."

I'm blinking back fury, trying to get ahold of myself and on the verge of punching him. "NO!"

Jason gets in my face, locking in as he says in a determined and ready to fight me if he needs to voice, "Face it. You're still hurt from when you watched what I did with Bernie. You were forced to sit there, unable to stop me or help me. And that was foreign to you, especially because you love me so much." His finger jams into my chest. "You're still scared for me in here. But I'm okay, Justin. It's not happening anymore. You don't have to protect me. It ended a long time ago *before Jake even met Drew*! That's how fuckin' long ago it was so you need to let this go. Talk to somebody, or write it out somewhere and burn the paper, I don't know. Whatever it takes until it's finally out of your system. Cry, punch something, scream in a dark alley, whatever it takes. But don't do this, Justin." He turns on his heel and walks away with that enigmatic statement in his wake.

I call after him, "Jason!" He stops. "Don't do what?"

"Don't come between your son and the woman he loves. Unless you want to lose him." Holding my look he walks inside, leaving me out here wondering how we switched places. I was always the wise one. I'm the older brother. By two minutes, sure, but that matters, dammit.

The problem with the truth is that when you hear it you can't ignore it. Some people try to stick their head back in the sand.

Me? Not so much.

PAIGE

M r. Cocker knocks on the doorframe, looking around to find I'm alone now. "Can I have a minute of your time, Paige?"

Bracing myself I nod, terrified. Nobody will tell me where Gabriel is, and I think he's why.

Mr. Cocker closes the door.

Oh God, here comes the gavel.

"Do you love my son?" he asks, meeting my scared eyes.

"Yes."

"Why?"

"Because he's a jerk," I whisper, before I realize that would be my answer.

Mr. Cocker's lips twitch. "Come again?"

"I mean, he's stubborn. Irritating. Um…"

Frowning and side-eyeballing me, Mr. Cocker says, "No, go on."

"He's petulant."

"Petulant?"

"He has a child's temper."

"I know what the word means, I just...never mind. Continue."

"He's extremely full of himself and sometimes doesn't think about how his actions impact other people."

"I see."

"And if I lost him, life would be so awful and so boring." Tears slide down my cheeks. "Gabriel makes me laugh. He surprises me. Pretty much everything he does is not what I would do. Sometimes when he's really mad he doesn't open the door for me and that keeps me on my toes, you know? It's not because he's being rude but because he's so passionate, and his moods take over his whole body so he can't control himself. He just explodes and runs off because his emotions are too much for him and he doesn't know how to handle them. But I've learned to see him being rude as a barometer for him needing to be heard. So I just listen and ask questions and try to get him back from the cliff he walked out on. He never knows I'm doing that. But he needs it. Like the day we were in Verona and he'd just called Ben for the millionth time, Gabriel ran around like he might punch someone so I flashed him, lifted up my shirt, when there were three old ladies behind me. It took him so much by surprise that his anger vanished just like that! And he just started laughing. Do you know how good that felt? I know how to help him. And he makes me feel safe. I've never felt safe before."

His father walks to the window and looks out, hands still stuffed away.

I think Elijah is right, they are alike.

Both are extremely guarded.

Or maybe discerning is the right word.

His voice is thoughtful as he says, "When Gabriel was a child he followed his brother everywhere, not the other way around. It was Elijah who led the way and I know that when he left for college, Gabriel was lost. He looked to my daughter, Hannah, for guidance but she was so used to ditching her younger brothers that she couldn't see he needed a friend." Mr. Cocker glances over and holds my eyes as he walks to the foot of my hospital bed. "Kids think their parents don't see things, but we do. It's the hardest part, that you have to let your kids stand on their own and choose their own paths. We have to let them fall on their faces, feel pain, so that they're able to handle it when life serves it to them. And also, so that when achievement comes they know the joy of having earned it. I'm not talking just about careers, although that's what I used to think mattered most. It doesn't." He pulls his hands from his pockets, one slides through his hair and the other dials his cell phone. "Excuse me while I send this text telling the hospital they can bring Gabriel here now."

Blinking at him I wait for the phone to be put away again. "You were keeping us apart."

"Yes."

"Why did you change your mind?"

He smiles for the first time, and it makes him seem far less scary. "Your reasons for loving my son...I wish my wife had been here to witness them." He chuckles to himself, "She would have described me in pretty much the same way when we met. But if the worst parts about him are what you consider the best, my doubts that you really do care for him are gone."

Gabriel's voice echoes from a distance, "Paige!" It gets louder as he keeps calling my name. "Paige! Paige!"

Mr. Cocker and I are watching the door. He doesn't move to answer it, just waits for Gabriel to explode through, dragging a rolling IV unit with him, wires dangling from his arm.

Seeing him, tears spring up. He glances to his father and rushes to me. He stops from cupping my face as he sees the bandages. Bending to inspect them he has such protective concern in his eyes. "You okay, Beautiful?" He traces my cheeks with gentle fingers.

"Now I am. Are *you* okay?"

"That fucking truck hit us! Why wasn't it on *my* side of the car?" he moans. "Not yours!"

"You should wear hospital gowns more often, Gabriel."

He stares at me, confused. Then starts laughing. "Stop it, it hurts to laugh! You like this? I had them give me two so my ass wasn't hanging out. Fucking humiliating." He kisses me and then presses our foreheads together. "I love you."

"I'm so crazy about you," I whisper.

Licking his lips he sits beside me and looks at his father, the shift in his expression powerful and quick. "Dad, I won't let you—"

"Stop. I only came in here to tell Paige I'm glad to see she's okay." Mr. Cocker meets my eyes and winks. "But if I knew I'd have to see all this sentimental bullshit I'd have waited outside." Rolling his eyes he strolls to the door. "Almost lost my lunch."

"Dad!" Gabriel calls out.

His father stops, head dropping as he sees Gabriel's face. "Not escaping that easily, am I."

"I know you kept me in that fucking hospital room just now. You can't do that shit anymore. Are you with me or against me? Because I'm going to marry Paige, Dad."

I gasp, "Gabriel!" because this is the first time I've heard him say that. He ignores me, waiting for his dad's answer.

Mr. Cocker's amusement vanishes. "I'm sorry I did that. It seems I have some demons from my past I have to face. Your mother brought that to my attention. But I've spoken with Paige and for what it's worth, not that you need it, I approve."

As my heart twists with relief and happiness, Gabriel stands up. "I do need it, Dad."

Mr. Cocker blinks away unexpected emotion, and his voice is gravelly as he says, "But you would've gone against my wishes anyway, had I not given you my approval."

"Yes."

A small smile flashes. "Then you're a man now." And with that he leaves.

Gabriel lets those words sink in before he walks around to the left side where I'm not bandaged up. Rolling his IV close he climbs in the bed with me and pulls the blanket over us. "Someday I want you to tell me what happened. Right now I just want to be with you."

"I want that, too." We adjust our bruised bodies to be able to snuggle. He kisses my forehead and we close our eyes.

Voices pass by in the hall. Nurses come check on us. But we don't move. Nothing matters now that we have each other again.

GABRIEL

One Month Later

*A*fter rinsing minty toothpaste out of my mouth in Carrie's bathroom, I ask, "You know what I've never done?"

Paige appears in the doorway, fastening her pink bra without effort. "Thought before you spoke? Said please?"

"Hardie har har," I dryly mutter as I flip her around and give her sweet ass a spank. "I've never had sex at one of our Family BBQs."

She rolls her eyes and walks away from me. "You've never brought a girl to one before, so how could you have?"

"I'm just saying! We could bang out two firsts today. If you'll excuse the awesome pun."

"The terrible pun."

"Awesome."

"Terrible."

Sliding up to her I smile down into her beautiful eyes. "Why do I let you give me so much shit all the time?"

She rises on her tiptoes and murmurs against my lips. "If you ever solve that mystery tell me so I can come up with a new one."

Grinning I unsnap her bra. "Oh no, look what happened."

"Gabriel," she laughs, grabbing the straps and wriggling away from my grasp. "We have to leave now. You need to put on some clothes because that is way too tempting." She points to my boxer briefs and the growing tent.

"We have to leave in five to...thirty minutes," I smirk, getting harder by the second.

She insists with firm head shaking, "Thirty?! No way!"

Sliding out of this confining cotton I lean against the wall and palm my cock as she walks to the closet to change her mind about the dress she wants to wear... for the fifth time.

Glancing over she sees what I'm doing and her eyelashes drop a little with lust. "Stop that."

But my hand keeps slowly stroking my length as I

start to throb. Closing my eyes a second I rasp, "I'm thinking of how wet you're getting."

Paige holds a dress up to her body, but her hungry eyes keep dropping down to watch. "What do you think of this one?"

"Too business like," I moan, bending my knees to squat here.

Her eyebrows go up. "That's an interesting position."

Thrusting my hips out a little, my profile is to her as I hold my cock on my open hand. "You sure you don't want to climb on?"

Her lips part as she stares at me. I can practically taste how turned on she is, and I'm getting off on knowing that. I start to grind my hips as I masturbate for our pleasure, putting on a real show. She swallows and drops the dress on the floor, walking to me and unsnapping her bra.

"Uh uh," I moan. "You have to touch yourself for me."

With shock her eyes widen slightly. "I've never done that in front of anyone!"

"Get on the bed."

Her mouth clamps shut at my tone. She climbs on the bed on all fours in just her pink panties, flipping her hair back to look at me over her shoulder.

I groan staring at her ass and the little bit of mound I can see of her pussy. "Nice try tempting me. Take off your panties."

She demurs, "Gabriel, I'm embarrassed."

"Take them off nice and slow."

Her eyelids get heavy and she kneels to slide her panties down her thighs, sitting down to wiggle out of them and set them on the bed.

"Spread your legs."

She swallows, nervous and excited as her knees separate. I groan as I gaze upon her pussy, getting off on the fact that I'm the only man who gets to see it.

"Show me how you like to pleasure yourself."

She whispers, "I'm scared," but her fingers are traveling over her onto the soft, dewy hair she let grow out for me. They slip beneath the cleft and tentatively start to play. Her breath hitches as I watch, stroking my cock in time with how she's touching herself. She bites her lip as she watches my fingers, then drops a quick gaze to her own. I rise up to stand over her and we lock eyes. I am dying with lust at the look I see in hers.

She's pulsing.

My cock is aching to fuck.

"I love you," I moan.

She whispers, glancing down, "I love you, too."

"Oh shit, that's it. I have to have you. You just said that to my cock." I dig my fingers into her hips and pull her ass to the edge of the bed. But she doesn't stop playing with herself. "Fuck yes," I moan as I position my tip against her. "You're dripping."

On a breathy moan she confesses, "Everything is throbbing!"

Pressing my erection into her inch by inch I groan at the sensation of her fingers tickling me while she keeps up the good work. Our mouths reach for each other and lock, tongues touching as I dive in and start pounding her. She moans in my mouth. I don't think I've ever been this hard in my life. Her free hand slams onto my back, fingernails digging in as she tears herself from my kiss and looks down to see everything we're doing.

"Oh, it's so hot," she gasp. "Harder! I'm going to cum. Fuck me harder. Harder!"

I do as she says and after eleven hard pumps her legs start shaking, pussy trembling before it slams against me with a steady heartbeat that rips my own orgasm, too. We crash together in a hot kiss as our bodies release the tension in hot spasms.

As the beat starts to slow down I gasp for air, blinking heavily. "You wreck me."

She smiles and traces my cheek with a touch so soft I close my eyes and lean into it, wishing for the first time in my life that I didn't have to go to the BBQ. I could just stay right here forever.

Gabriel's new, black, electric Ferrari is as quiet as a feather floating across the ground as we glide up to his grandparent's home in Buckhead. He parks and strolls around to help me out. I'm sitting here dutifully waiting while I stare at the green expanse of lawn that leads to their beautiful and enormous house. Taking his hand I stand up but can't take my eyes off their front door. It's open and people are walking inside, a few waving to him and calling out, "Hi Gabriel!"

"That's my Grandpa's sister, Marie. She's married to him, Don, who used to own the construction company...You know what. Fuck it." He leads me to the driveway so we don't walk on this bright green, expertly trimmed grass. "Don't even try to memorize their names today. Too fucking many. Just smile and nod."

Laughing under my breath from nerves and a strong desire to run, I tell him, "I'm glad you suggested the long summer dress. If I'd worn the knee-length one I'd feel more...exposed. Especially after what we just did."

He kisses my fingers. "You look beautiful."

"You're not going to punch Ben, are you?"

Gabriel's eyes flicker. "I said I wouldn't."

"But why won't you promise?"

"Because I don't want to break it."

Tugging on his fingers I try to impress upon him that I really need this to go smoothly, but he ignores my signal and goes to hug his sister. She smiles at me and comes in for a hug. "I was just holding Kaya and I told my husband I can't wait anymore. I need one!"

Smiling I agree, "Kaya's so cute, Hannah. I don't blame you."

Gabriel's still got the edge in his voice as he asks, "Ben here?"

She answers no, without noticing the tension. Her mind is still full of rattles and strollers. "We've been trying but it just hasn't happened yet."

Gabriel's intense grip is stopping the blood in my fingers. Smiling with a hint of pain I say, "It'll happen for you guys. Don't worry, Hannah. Maybe the worrying is stopping the flow of energy." I glance to my boyfriend who doesn't get the message.

"Ben's not here yet?" he asks again.

Hannah frowns, "No, if you want to see him so badly why don't you call and ask where he is."

"Because he doesn't return fucking phone calls!" Gabriel barks, tugging me inside.

Hannah calls after us, "What the hell was that?"

"He's hungry," I tell her over my shoulder. "Just have to get him some of that amazing chili he keeps telling me about."

He's not looking for food. What he's really doing is searching the house just in case she was wrong. But as I'm introduced to cousins, aunts and uncles, Gabriel's hand relaxes and his smile comes easily again.

Here he isn't the celebrity he is with the general public. His family treats him like the boy they grew up with, and I can't get enough of his laugh as they give him a hard time. He volleys back their joking insults, but with his aunts he shows nothing but respect.

They're such a great family, so filled with humor, that my nerves disappear and I'm laughing more often than not, completely forgetting that I'm new here. They open their arms to me in a way that's kind of amazing.

As Max, Caden and Gabriel are huddled together talking about who knows what, Mrs. Cocker brings me a glass that looks like a smokier lemonade, a knowing smile on her strikingly beautiful face. "You have to try this. It's legendary."

Taking a sip I react, "Mmmm! Oh my God, what is it?"

"Nancy's fresh ginger-ale. There are stories that Jason used to drink it all before anyone could have some. He would hide the pitcher!"

"Sounds like Gabriel. He steals food from my plate all the time!"

With her usual poise she covers a mother's curiosity. "So how are things going with you two?"

"He's wonderful, Mrs. Cocker."

"Are you thinking of moving in together soon?"

"Um…I just found another job and I want to wait a little while so we don't rush."

I can tell this impresses her. "Hmm," she smiles and pauses as she hears her husband calling her name. "Near the base of the porch, Justin!"

He strolls down the three steps, eyeing his son and nephews as he walks to join us. "Paige, what do you think of the house I grew up in?"

"It's beautiful. I love that it's not a museum."

He cocks his head. "How's that?"

Self-conscious, I slowly explain, "Um…from the outside it looks very intimidating, but inside it's cozy and homey. Like you and your brothers didn't have to worry about breaking something and getting in trouble. There was room for you to be boys."

Huffing through his nose he glances to his wife. "Insightful, this one."

Mrs. Cocker nods and mutters from behind her glass, "Thank God Gabriel didn't bring home a trashy groupie."

Justin laughs and shows us that amazing smile again, the one I glimpsed in the hospital room. I think because it's so rare it has an even greater impact. But then he locks eyes with me and asks, "How's your brother?"

My heart quickens as I glance down for a second. "He went to a couple meetings, but he's out again."

Mr. Cocker nods, lips tightening in thought as he glances to his family. "Well, that's improvement. Let's just pray that he finds his way back in the rooms soon." I give him a grateful smile before he walks away to yell at his brother, "Jason, what the fuck are you doing with all that corn bread?"

"Language!" comes a shockingly loud yet genteel southern drawl.

Gabriel hurries over. "Oh shit, I forgot to introduce you to Grams." He takes his mother's glass from her hands and downs it, handing it back to her. "Thanks, Mom."

She and I exchange a shocked look. "Gabriel! The whole thing! I thought you'd just take a sip!"

He gives her a lopsided smile. "When have I ever had just a sip?" Taking my hand he guides me away but not before I hand my glass to her and she gives me the empty one. "Hey!" he cries out.

"I've got your back, Mrs. Cocker!"

"Thank you, Paige," she laughs.

Gabriel grumbles, "Gonna have to come up with

some new tactics," as he guides me to a sweet old lady sitting atop two cushions on the long bench. "Grams, this is my future wife, Paige Miller."

"Oh my Gosh," I mumble, embarrassed at his bold announcement. He does these things just to watch me squirm. "Hi, Mrs. Cocker. We're not officially engaged."

"Call me Grams. Everybody does." She shakes my hand with fragile fingers, a sharp gleam in her eyes. "Paige, do you know what you're getting into with this one?"

"Yes. Unfortunately."

The inspection she's giving me melts into a warm smile. "Oh good, she's witty. She can stay."

Gabriel laughs with me, but his is louder and very proud. I didn't know it until now, but his heart needed her to say that. "Grams is the reason we're all here. She and my great grandpa Jerald fell in love during World War II."

"Wow," I breathe, eyes wide. "Are you a vampire? Your skin is amazing!"

Her cheeks flush light pink and she touches her chest. "Well, aren't you sweet." To Gabriel she smiles, "I think she meant that!"

"She did." He winks and squeezes my hand. "Paige is a little *too* honest."

"Well then I will take that compliment home with me! Oh look, Ben is here! And he brought a date, too! What a lucky day we're having."

Gabriel and I turn our heads.

Ben is strolling out to join everyone in the back-yard. His hand is clasped with Shelby's.

*B*en spots me and stiffens, but he's overrun with people greeting him. Of course everyone is surprised as fuck to see him with a date for the first time. Nobody comes to a Cocker BBQ unless they're family, in-laws, or they're going to marry one of us. It's an unspoken thing evolved over the years because of a lot of reasons.

So why the fuck is he here with Shelby?

Paige is more shocked than I am. "What happened to Carter?" she asks, as we watch them make the rounds. "She was living with her boyfriend!"

"Guess Carter is in the dust somewhere. You still haven't talked to her, right?"

Stunned she says, "No, when I quit Jordanna's studio she was cold to me. I told her to call when she was ready to be my friend again. She never did."

I say through gritted teeth, "Guess she was busy," eyeing my tall cousin as he dwarfs the others.

He can't hide and he's not trying to.

His green eyes keep locking with mine.

He knows a storm is coming.

Elijah appears in the doorway. For the casual occasion he's ditched the suit for some grey slacks and a white button-up. He's got his hands in his pockets, classic Cocker cover for unease. He scans the yard, seeing Ben first and by the look in his eyes that's why Elijah came outside. He must have heard the commotion from Grandpa's office where he was working until the absolute last minute.

But now work has to be put on hold.

Searching for me he gives me an almost imperceptible nod.

Ethan stands up, handing his baby to his CEO wife, Charlie, with a tense smile for her that disappears as he looks at me.

So Ben told him about us.

Just like I thought, talking behind my back.

I'm going to fucking kill him.

"Gabriel," Paige desperately says as I head in their direction. There are at least thirty people scattered throughout the backyard and kitchen. Some by the long food table, some down by the old dolphin fountain that no longer works. Some laughing as they carry out pitchers and dishes.

Grandpa Michael is greeting Shelby with a warm smile as Grandma Nance is chatting her up.

So I wait. Ethan waits. Elijah strolls down the stairs.

As soon as our grandparents step away from Ben he sees me, and Shelby's nervous smile disappears. I jerk my head to the side of the porch where we can talk. He nods.

My fingers let go of Paige. "Wait here."

"No!" She grabs on and tightens her hold. "Don't do anything!"

With my jaw twitching I lead her over. Ethan's face is cool and collected trying to broadcast to the rest of the family that nothing is happening.

Elijah isn't even trying to mask it.

He's as grim as I am.

Shelby is staring at Paige, and her back is extra straight. My girl is about to ask what's going on but I cut her off, voice low. "You can't return a fuckin' phone call?"

He's just as quiet, but not nearly as angry. Calm motherfucker that he is. "After you ditched me at Ray's?"

Elijah is on my left, Paige on my right. I let go of her hand and growl at Ben, "You tried to steal my date! You showed up at the fuckin' restaurant thinking you could take her!"

Glaring at me he growls back, "You hadn't even met her yet. How was I supposed to know that the one time you'd actually commit to something it'd be now!?"

My fist flies out.

I punch him so hard he reels back.

Shelby yells, "Ben!"

Paige cries, "No!"

And that's it.

The BBQ goes dead silent.

Ethan gets in between us but Elijah grabs him so I can do what I've gotta do. Ben comes at me and we start brawling. Fists landing where they have to. Family shouting at the top of their lungs for us to stop. My Dad and Uncle Jason work to get me off of Ben.

Ben's dad, Uncle Jaxson growls, "Enough!" and pushes his son back twice as he tries to come at me for more.

Uncle Jake and Uncle Jeremy get in the middle.

My dad and his twin have my arms and are ordering me to stand down.

Grandpa Michael tears Elijah's hands off Ethan's T-shirt and rips it. "What is the matter with all of you?" he bellows to the four of us, his patriarchal presence taking up the whole yard just like that. "Will someone ·tell me what is going on?"

Panting, Ben and I glare at each other.

Everyone waits for an explanation.

It won't come.

My mom and Ben's mom, Aunt Rachel, rush in between the two groups of testosterone, their arms out like they don't want to get hit if someone gets free.

Aunt Rachel says, "Are we going to get an explanation for this?"

"Or are you going to keep acting like animals?" Mom looks at my girl. "Paige, you want to enlighten us?"

Instantly I'm protective of her but as usual she can take care of herself. Shaking her head once she boldly says, "If Gabriel doesn't want to say, then I won't force him. This is between them."

My father huffs through his nose but I know he respects what she just did, despite how much it irritates him not to have the reason.

He and Jason let me go with warning looks.

I shake myself out, adjusting my shirt and cutting a quick glance around the party. Well, it was a party. Not so much one now.

Ben runs his hands through his hair and nods to his father that he's under control, leave him alone. Jaxson's nostrils flare but he takes a step back.

My brother's voice booms out, surprising us all. "Now that it's over, can we put this behind us? Or is everyone going to whisper all night long? Are we children or are we Cockers?"

Grandpa Michael regards Elijah with a cool expression, a glint of respect in his eyes for taking charge like he just did. The younger cousins take the cue, nodding and saying they're Cockers.

If Uncle Jett was here this would not be dropped so

easily, so I'm glad he's not. Same with Sofia Sol. She'd be shouting for an explanation.

And a resolution we're not ready for.

The group disperses but makes sure that Ben and I are not near each other at the table. Hannah tells Elijah to scoot over so she can sit by me, Paige on my other side. Tobias is next to my twin, his mouth tight.

Hannah whispers as everyone tries to have a normal BBQ, "I had to hold Tobias back. He's a pro fighter — he would've hurt Ben more than you wanted him to."

"Don't be too sure about that."

"You need to let this go. You won." She locks eyes with Paige.

Inhaling patience I say, "Maybe someday I will, Hannah. But not today."

"Gabriel," she whispers.

"All he had to do was pick up a phone."

That shuts her up.

GABRIEL

*A*s the party winds down, Ben is nowhere to be found. I've left Paige with Mom, telling them I was going to the bathroom when I wasn't.

Dad and Uncle Jaxson corner me in the hallway and we all walk into Grandpa Michael's office, family photos on every wall. Elijah had snuck in here to finish emailing, so he rises from Grandpa's chair as soon as we walk in.

Jaxson informs me, "I already made Ben take his girlfriend home before another fight broke out. He was looking for you, too."

Dad glowers at me. "You want to tell us what the fuck happened between you?"

"He tried to take Paige from me!"

They exchange a look and Dad mutters, "He gets it from you."

Jaxson grates, "Fuck you, Justin. That's not funny." Locking onto me he says, "Tell me the story."

I give them the abbreviated one. Elijah nods at certain points when they look at him. When I'm done they're silent and process it.

Jaxson clarifies, "Shelby was Paige's best friend?"

"Yup."

"She was with them the night I got her money back," Dad tells the room while concentrating on how to fix this. "That's probably what brought them together."

I snort with heavy sarcasm. "Oh really? Because he had Paige at his house when I called from London! Shelby is his consolation prize. Probably just called her up 'cause he didn't know how to handle rejection for the first time!"

Jaxson's nostrils flare as he glares at me, protective of his only child. "You need to get a hold of yourself."

"No, I don't! Nothing wrong with being pissed when you're treated like this. I gave him plenty of chances to talk to me and he never called me back!"

Dad crosses his arms. "Your ditching him at that restaurant wasn't exactly grown-up behavior."

I shove my hands in my pockets. "Whatever."

They look at each other. Nobody has a solution. Jaxson shakes his head. "Someone's gotta fix this."

A light knocking on the slightly open door makes us all turn our heads. Paige is there, her soothing voice low and respectful. "I'd like to try to talk to Ben."

"No way!"

"Gabriel, let me help."

"No!"

She looks angelic in her gentle patience as she tilts her head a little. "This is all because of ego, so more ego won't fix it, I'm sorry."

My dad and uncle look at each other like they can see why this fight happened in the first place. "You plan to mediate this, Paige?"

"Yes, Mr. Cocker. I think if we just discuss this like adults it will all be put to rest."

Dad claps a hand on Jaxson's shoulder, making a joke for him not to try and take Paige, too. "Sorry buddy, my son called dibs."

Jaxson chuckles, "Jackass," and follows him out of the room.

Elijah and I share a look, wondering what private joke or story they know about that we don't.

Paige shuts the door. "Come with me to his farm, Gabriel. I need to talk to Shelby, too." She takes my hand. "Please do this for me."

"Just say yes," Elijah mutters, heading back to the desk. "I've got a mess on my hands I need to get back to."

"Oh, sorry for getting in the way of your ambition."

"Shut it," he chuckles as we all leave Grandpa's favorite room.

PAIGE

The Ferrari's tires spit gravel as we drive up Ben's driveway. He's standing on the porch, Shelby leaning against the wall behind him. Everyone looks like somebody died, because when you fight with people you love, a piece of you is dead until you can heal the rift.

"Promise you'll let me do the talking until you're calm." I slide my fingers up Gabriel's arm in the tenderest way I can.

With his eyes locked on his cousin he mutters, "Promise," and turns off the ignition, jumping out to open my door.

My instinct is to leap out now just in case they're going to go at it, but I know better. He needs to show that I'm his. Opening my door and offering his hand is the gentlemanly way that men are taught to behave. It's a show of respect for both of us. But I'm shaking.

When my fingers slide onto his, he notices and his body loses the tension a bit in order to calm me down.

"Thank you for meeting us," I smile.

Ben nods. "No problem."

Gabriel bites back a sarcastic remark which shows great restraint on his part.

Shelby takes a couple deep breaths. She looks like she belongs out here in this quiet place. Her blonde curls are wild, no makeup save for a hint of pink on her lips. Her jeans and yellow, cotton blouse fit right in with Ben's no-frills style.

We take a seat at the round table he set on the porch. I'm sure they've spent mornings here together, sharing life stories over coffee after nights with little sleep.

Shelby pours us all glasses from a pitcher of sweet tea, as if she's been here forever. When she places mine down I see she's shaking, too. We lock eyes but only for a second before she sits and starts picking at her nails. Ben and Gabriel are stiff and quiet across from each other. It's boy girl, boy girl.

Did she go to Ben for the same reason I did? Because she needed his strength? I bet it was her who sought him out because Carter wasn't equipped to deal with how shaken she was after what happened. Shelby hasn't seen the darkness I have from growing up in the shadow of addiction. She was always bubbly and silly… and maybe more fragile than I ever realized.

I take a sip of tea, clear my throat and begin. "When

we first got to your family's BBQ I was overwhelmed. But then everybody was so nice and...they laugh so much and are so close!" Ben and Gabriel shift in their chairs at the reminder. "I got a glimpse of how magical what you guys have, is. That you would fight and throw that away is a tragedy. I think what happened is a terrible misunderstanding. You guys love each other, you both know that." Touching Gabriel's arm to let him know I'm his and this is all for him, I glance to his cousin and say, "Ben, I know that's why you didn't call. You didn't know what to say, how to explain yourself. It was probably embarrassing, wasn't it? So that made it really hard to talk to him about it." I turn to my boyfriend, stroking his arm. "And Gabriel, you're hurt because you feel left out so often. And traveling all the time doesn't help. That feeling got triggered when you felt ignored by Ben, who you've always looked up to. It had to hurt. And not just a little bit, but a lot."

His eyes drop to the table as Ben stares at him, clearly surprised at learning something new.

"I'm sure Shelby is wondering what's so special about me."

I hold her guarded eyes as they go wide. That's what's been gnawing at her. I can only imagine how it feels to be her in this circumstance.

"This isn't about me, Shelbs. Ben was ready to meet someone...because I think he was looking for you. It was so obvious as we drove up and I saw you two, how much you belong here. Maybe that's why he ran into me that day, so you guys would meet. Then it all went wonky. You don't have to worry. This fighting isn't over me, it's become about them — just two guys who got angry and had no idea how to talk about their feelings. It happens to men all the time." I pause and offer her an apologetic smile. "And we're no exception, right?"

"Paige," she whispers, wiping her cheeks.

Ben protectively reaches for her hand and their fingers entwine as she gives him a grateful smile.

He looks at me, frowning, "Fuck."

Gabriel chuckles with the hurt still tinting his voice. "Yeah, Paige does that." He leans over to give me a quick kiss. "Cut us all wide open, why don't you?"

Shelby laughs through her tears, "Ever thought of being a shrink?"

Choked up, too, I laugh and hold her eyes. "I miss you, Shelbs."

Her cute face squishes up and she croaks, "I miss you, too!" She leaps out of the chair and hurries over to melt into my arms. We rock each other, crying.

Ben and Gabriel sit there, awkward and silent.

"I have some whiskey."

Gabriel shoots up from his chair. "I'm in."

Shelby and I crack up laughing from the release of all that tension as we follow the boys inside.

*W*hen I wake up in Ben's guest room with a headache that makes me swear never to drink that much ever again, I blink over to the empty side of the bed.

Padding barefoot into the hall I see the door to Ben's room closed, and head downstairs to find my boyfriend.

The sound of his and his cousin's voices slows my steps. Through the front window I see them at the round table, dawn's golden-blue sunlight on their faces as they easily talk with one another while sipping coffee.

I can't hear them, but Gabriel hasn't looked that stress-free since I met him, so I tiptoe upstairs and climb back into bed.

When I'm awoken by his kisses I don't know how

long I was out. Slipping my arms around his neck I smile, "Morning, Handsome."

"Hey, Beautiful," he smiles back. "Marry me."

Quietly laughing like he's crazy I kiss him again.

He pulls away and says, "I'm serious. I don't have the ring with me, but we'll pick it out together. You were so amazing last night and I can't go another day without telling you I need you as my wife. I know I've mentioned it before, but I'm flat out asking you now. Will you marry me?"

Searching his kaleidoscope eyes I see love and honesty shining from them. "We're so young."

"So were Romeo and Juliet."

"Look how that turned out."

He ducks his head in my neck, shoulders shaking with laughter. Rising up to lock eyes with me again he says, "Even with my proposal you're giving me a hard time."

"Only because you love it," I smirk. "But really, we're so young."

"One thing you probably don't know about my family, Paige, is that when we find who we want, we don't fuck around." His hand dips into my panties and he cups me and murmurs against my lips. "I want you. I knew it when I saw you. Love at first sight is real, rare but real. I know because I had it with you." He pauses and smirks at me. "Even if it took you a little longer to catch up."

Grinning at him I roll us over so that I'm sitting on

top of him, bending down to whisper and keep this conversation private. "But I said I love you first, so we're even." He cocks his head to tell me he's waiting for an answer. "Yes, I'll marry you. But I want to wait to have babies."

"What?" He flips me back over, his sexy hair falling in front of his frown. "Why?"

"I want it to just be us for a little while."

An amazing smile lights his face up. "Deal. We're getting you on the pill when we get back to Atlanta. And Carrie's going to have to find a new tenant." He kisses me before whispering, "But then I want at least four kids."

Warmth drifts into my chest. "When enough time passes I'll give you anything you want, Gabriel. Anything."

We gaze at each other until a smirk tugs at him. "You're such a pain in my ass."

Laughing I snuggle closer. "And you say the sweetest things."

He chuckles and kisses my head. "You're not going to let me fuck you in Ben's guest room, are you?"

"Not a chance."

GABRIEL

Four years later

I stroll into *Om This* and hear that peaceful music I always give my wife so much shit for every time I come here. Other than that the place feels empty. "Beautiful! Where are you?"

She calls from the restrooms, "Lock the door for me! I'll be right out!"

Digging my keys from my pocket I shuffle through them to find the one that belongs to this store and not the other two we expanded with last year. "You changing clothes for dinner?"

"Yep! Be right out!"

Shelby clued us in on the fact that the business was up for sale when Jordanna finally told herself she didn't even like yoga. Paige insists on working even though we don't need the money.

Human beings need to feel useful.

If we don't we go insane.

As usual I couldn't argue with her logic.

Especially after Bobby went back to school to study engineering. It kept his mind occupied and his teacher is the inspiring kind who makes his students respect him because he engages them in new ways. Bobby wanted to impress him, so he worked harder. Then he stopped falling off the wagon and got a sponsor. But my dad still won't let him come to the Family BBQs.

I'm not a huge fan of Paige running three stores, since I'm a narcissist and want her to myself all the time. But what I could do was hire a large staff so she can skip town whenever I need her to travel with me, and of course she's always game.

Shelby stopped teaching yoga classes long ago. She does the books for us, but other than that she stays up north working the organic farm with her husband Ben. Weirdest thing to watch her and my cousin get married. But whatever.

I turn the sign over in the window as I've done countless times, and wait by the register checking my phone and eyeing the speakers. "Fuck it," I mutter, walking to scroll through her playlist and put something else on.

To make her laugh I almost choose my own music and act like it's the only thing I listen to, when she knows that's bullshit. It'd be fun to fuck with her, though. But on second thought I hit the R&B list for Otis Redding's song, *These Arms of Mine.*

Paige calls out from the back studio room. "I love this song!"

"How'd you get back there?" I call back, confused as to how I missed her.

"I snuck."

"You *snuck*?" Growing curious my steps pick up speed and I turn the corner with my hand on the doorframe, pausing as I see candles spread out around a spread of fluffy blankets. "Those are from home."

"Very good detective work, Sherlock," she smiles, walking out from the storage room in a black negligee that makes my cock start filling up right away.

"Oh wow, Happy Birthday to me."

She's got heels on even though there's a no-shoes allowed rule in this room. "Figured I'd give you your present before we go eat." Biting her lip in the sexiest way, she slips a spaghetti strap down her shoulder, letting it hang there where my teeth want to get at it. She bends over and gracefully lands on her hands in Downward-Facing Dog position.

"Oh, you gotta be kidding me," I groan, unzipping my pants.

"The door is locked for a reason. Take it all off."

Hissing through my teeth I undress as she cranes her ass higher in the air to tease me.

"I've always wondered what it would feel like to

fuck you in that position when you're half-enlightened."

Stifling a laugh, Paige says, "Look back there."

I stand behind her and see the crotch has a snap release. "Oh, man, best birthday gift ever."

"Thought you'd like that," she whispers with sex in her voice. I pop the thing open with two fingers and slide one up her pussy.

"You're so wet, Beautiful. Guess knowing you were going to surprise me got you all excited, huh?" I bend down and lick her. She pushes into my mouth and gives this breathy moan that makes me even harder. "You know what's going to happen, don't you? Every time you do this position in class from now on you're going to imagine my cock pressing up in you like this. Filling you. Stretching you. Making your whole torso catch fire as I take you from behind and massage your ass like this. Trace my fingers over your lower back and thighs just like this. Thrust *real* slowly until you beg me to go faster. That's right. Moan a little louder, wife. Nobody can hear you." As I angle my hips and start pounding her I rasp, "Go ahead and make those sexy little noises when you lose control."

She starts rubbing into me and moans, "Gabriel! Keep talking!"

"You like it when I talk dirty? You like me to describe how that sweet heat builds inside you. How it threatens to turn you inside out it feels so good. You're pulsing on my cock. Mmm, so fucking tight. So wet." I grab her hips and go to town.

She moans and her voice just does me in. I need to kiss her.

Bending over I wrap my arms around her and lift up, kissing her right shoulder blade as I fuck her standing. She grabs my head, twisting her torso to be able to kiss me. Our tongues dance as we move. Panting she breaks free, locks eyes with me and whispers, "I'm pregnant. Happy Birthday, Handsome."

I freeze.

"What? Really?"

Laughing with happiness she nods. I pull out in an instant to lay her down on the blankets, underneath me, diving in from here where I can see her eyes and every facial expression she makes.

She starts crying as I hold inside her body. My tears mingle with hers and I kiss her.

Touching my face she whispers, "We're going to have a baby, Gabriel. *Are you ready for this?*"

She made me wait four years.

Because she knew.

I wasn't ready when I met her.

Not even when I proposed.

Or when we walked down the aisle.

But now we own these three businesses together, have toured the world with my music and for fun, have fallen more in love as the years have passed, and we've grown up.

No, that isn't right.

When I met her she was already a grown-up, so wise beyond her years.

It's me who became a man finally. And I did it with her patience holding me up every single day until I stood as tall as she saw me to be.

I smile into my wife's beautiful eyes. "With all of my heart, body and soul, Paige...*I'm ready.*"

The End.

NOTE FROM ME

(TURN THE PAGE FOR THE GOODIES.)

I wasn't sure who would be the next star of series. It was either Eric or Gabriel. If you've read the bonus scenes you can get online by joining my club, you know it could not have been Ben. His love story has to come later.

Gabriel kept pulling at me. So I started to type. I don't plot out stories—I let the characters take me where they want to. When Ben ran into Paige I thought…uh oh. Triangle time, and how is this going to end? It got hairy and I bit my lips until they chapped.

Especially because I knew this would cause some readers to want to slap me. Sometimes (often) my books don't go the way you guys expect and believe me, I hear about it. But I can't help but be honest for my characters. Ben acted like a jerk. So did Gabriel. Many times over. He was still a boy when he found his forever. What are you gonna do? Run off and ditch your hot, older cousin I guess, before he wins her from you. hahaha.

And Paige should have told Shelby about Bobby, or should she? Her parents shouldn't have left her alone to deal with him...except she made the choice to do that on her own, didn't she?

It's all subjective.

But so exciting!

I googled *Om This* and found out it doesn't exist, so I bought the domain name and will probably make some fun merchandise with it. We shall see!

Every book in this series is so different from each other that I'm sure you're scratching your head sometimes wondering what I'm going to do next. But don't ask me. Ask them.

And while we're at it...hey, Eric, are you the star of the next book? Or is Emma going to sneak in there first?

Like you, dear reader, I can't wait to find out.

xx,
Faleena Hopkins

THANK YOU TO THE READERS...

...who helped me name some of the characters for this book!

My Read&Review Pack had the honor of helping me name our leading ladies *Paige* and *Shelby*.

And in the **Cocky Readers Facebook Group**, my *#CockerStalkers* helped me out with some fun yoga research. They didn't know I wasn't going to do this until after all their comments came in — I took every one of the commenter's names for characters in the *Om This* scenes. It is my way of thanking them for being a part of the online conversation.

The 'villains' Jordanna and Ms. Bauer aren't named after readers. ;)

And a huge thank you to my proofing team for their attention to detail and for putting up with my wackiness this go-around: Teri F., Linda M., Tally G., Hopey G. and Julie R.

Thank you, ladies, for being part of the journey!

xx, Faleena Hopkins

Special Bonus Scenes

Now available in Paperback: the collection of "future scenes" for the Cocker Brothers series, Books 1-16 together. These all take place after *"The End."*

Links to:
YouTube Cover Model Interviews
Cocky Bookmarks
Signed Paperbacks
Cocker Family Tree
Spotify — Series Playlists
Hot Instagram
http://authorfaleenahopkins.com

Facebook Group
(search:) Cocky Readers: Cocker Brothers
Purely for true #cockerstalkers

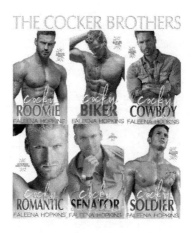

Series in Chronological Order:

(Can be enjoyed out of sequence)

Cocky Roomie - Jake Cocker

Cocky Biker - Jett Cocker

Cocky Cowboy - Jaxson Cocker

Cocky Romantic - Jason Cocker

Cocky Senator - Justin Cocker

Cocky Soldier - Jeremy Cocker

A Honey Badger X-Mas (Cocky Biker spinoff)

Cocky Senator's Daughter - Hannah Cocker

Cocky Genius - Ethan Cocker

Cocky Rockstar - Gabriel Cocker

Cocky Love - Emma Cocker

Cocky Quarterback - Eric Cocker

Cocky Rebel - Sofia Sol Cocker

Cocky By Association - Sean & Celia

Cocky Director - Max Cocker

Cocky and Out of My League - Nicholas Cocker

Cocky Bonus Scenes: Book 1-16

(more coming!)

Not in the Cocky Series

You Don't Know Me

A stand alone novel

Paranormal Romance

Werewolves of New York

Werewolves of Chicago

Owned by The Alphas

ABOUT THE AUTHOR

 I've been writing since I was six-years-old when I sold my parents books for a dollar, written in crayon, hand illustrated to the best of my limited abilities, and bound with yarn by tiny, nail-bitten fingers.

Now today I'm also a filmmaker and actress. Stay tuned for the first feature film I'll be directing. The men have been doing that for decades (Woody Allen, Ben Affleck, Ed Burns, to name a few who act in their own projects), so why not give it a shot? I hope you'll be at my side for that. Should be a roller coaster of crazy.

Love, love, and more love,

xx,
Faleena Hopkins

Still curious about me? Here's my heart on my sleeve in a memoir blog post:

http://faleenahopkins.blogspot.com/2017/04/from-atlanta-to-new-york-city.html

Made in the USA
Middletown, DE
12 May 2018